VINTAGE TALES

# COUNTRY OF COLD

Vintage Tales

# COUNTRY

# KEVIN PATTERSON

*Kevin Patter—*
6·6·05

# OF COLD

STORIES *of* SEX *and* DEATH

VINTAGE CANADA

www.randomhouse.ca

Some of the stories in the book have appeared, in different form, in the following publications: "Gabriella: Parts One and Two" and "Insomnia, Infidelity, and
the Leopard Seal" in *Canadian Fiction Magazine*, "The Perseid Shower" in *Prairie
Fire*, and "Interposition" in *Toronto Life magazine*.

### National Library of Canada Cataloguing in Publication

Patterson, Kevin, 1964–
    Country of cold / Kevin Patterson.

(Vintage tales)
ISBN 0–679–31046–0
   I. Title. II. Series.

PS8581.A7886C69 2003        C813.'6       C2002–904399–9
PR9199.4.P38C69 2003

*Book design by* CS Richardson
Printed and bound in Canada

2 4 6 8 9 7 5 3 1

*This book is for Torvald*

# CONTENTS

Vintage Tales

Flight paths stretch through the air of the northern prairie, defining the place as much as the striped cultivated plain below them does. Great skeins of Canada, snow, and blue geese cross the sky in the spring and autumn. All year round, jets twinkle their way back and forth to the cities on the edges of the continent, and to European cities where there is more of a different kind of beauty. These cities are not, sensibly, the destination of the geese; they shuttle their way between the Arctic and the wheat and rice fields of the southern prairie, opposite poles on an axis that is itself the polar opposite of the cities on the edges of the continent.

For the geese, and every other prairie dweller, the Arctic has a complex appeal. It is an extension, an exaggerated version, of the prairie, similarly treeless and lonely. The devastated beauty of the Arctic is contained within the idea of the prairie. The difference is only that the prairie has enough summer for topsoil to form. For those drawn to the prairie, the Arctic is irresistible, and for those who face away from the prairie, it is unthinkable. The geese go north to nest and to feed, and find the tundra bounteous. The loneliness of the place suits their purposes. There are few predators there, and from the top of even a small hillock, one can see for miles.

Loneliness is as much a feature of topography as are wetlands and ridges and eskers. Certain creatures dwell naturally in it, and others are propelled from it. The flight paths over this part of the world reach toward and away from the topography of absence: this place can be home, but it will still cast one out.

# LES IS MORE

It was a Tuesday when Lester came home from work, five in the morning and the sky bled pale in the east, trailer empty. Rhonda gone, gone, gone. Lester sat down on their bed and looked at the drawers still pulled open and the detritus of fast packing. The carpet was flaked with torn paper and the rising sun lit the pressboard-panelled walls with an oblique and brightening glow. Lester felt like detritus himself. Then he got back into his truck and drove down to the Billy Burger Drive-Thru. He ate a triple Billy Buster Burger and two orders of onion rings and a piece of apple pie and an ice cream cone. Then he went home and slept. When he woke up in the afternoon he went down to Flora's Café and ate steak and eggs. Then French toast. And a milkshake. And another piece of apple pie.

In the months that followed, Lester gained a half-dozen track suits and the profile of an engorged chigger. Never in his life had he been more than routinely bulbous. Now, when he stood straight and naked and looked down, he could barely see his penis from above. He shook his pendulous arms and watched them jiggle.

In the mirror, behind his burgeoning girth, he could see milkshake cups stacked on the table beside his bed. Walking through the house: in the kitchen the dishes leaned drunkenly and the takeout menu of every restaurant within thirty miles that had a delivery van was taped to the refrigerator door. He had not spoken much with Rhonda since she left, although he had seen her in town a few times, where they both had looked frightened and alarmed at one another. Her lawyer had written him a letter a few months ago. After he read it he had cried for about an hour, hanging on to the door handle of the freezer compartment. If things continued at this pace, soon he would not be able to turn around behind the bar down at the Rushing River Bar and Grill.

Fridays, when college is in session, the Rushing River howls with adolescent fury; mascara runs like rained-on fresh paint, cotton ribbed T-shirts cling to magnificent shoulders, and there are always some who can't wait to get home. Angry music hollers and so does Lester: Beer is two and a quarter I said! And get your ass off the bar!

Bud and Double Diamond on tap! Thank you!" Lester and his friend Cindee, one of the waitresses, keep up a running repartee of deranged facial expressions. Cocked eyebrows, crossed eyes and pre-emetic cheek bulging has them entertained and at least a little distracted from youth, half in the bag.

On this night, Marilyn, the head waitress, was in a foul mood, and when it was this busy the kids made her steadily fiercer and Cindee was hiding from her. Apparently there had been words. Cindee's absence only increased the number of belligerent and beer-breathed children thrusting their faces into Marilyn's and the coming cataclysm was one well-trod path. Lester decided that tonight it would be worth the price of defusing the Cindee-Marilyn thing and maybe not getting hit with flying crockery. Lester got Harold, the bouncer, to watch the bar for a minute, which Harold never minded, as he felt it gave him licence to steal as much of Lester's tips as he could fit in his too-tight jeans pockets.

First Lester checked the stairs below the kitchen and listened for weeping. Then he went into the kitchen and asked Donna, the cook, if she had seen Cindee. Finally he climbed the stairs to the roof and looked out. He sat down on a ventilation shaft and panted. The sky was very clear and very black. The roof shook from the music. The ventilation shaft shook from Lester. When he finally caught his breath he heard the soft mewing of

Cindee crying. He stood up and followed the sound through the maze of ventilation ducts on the rooftop. He sat down beside her. She was holding a bottle of Molson Canadian between her legs and looking off toward the falls. "Hey," he said, wheezing.

"Hey yourself," she said, between sobs. The floodlights were shining purple and green against the falling water and they both studied them.

"She's cranky, hey?"

"Who?"

"Marilyn."

"No, she's fine." Cindee and Les sat there. The music thumped below them and the Rushing River Falls roared faintly at the edge of town.

"So . . . you thought you'd set down your tray in the middle of a set and come up here because . . ."

"I feel awful, Les."

"How come?"

"I gotta move out from Sam, I think." Sam her live-in boyfriend of the last three years, quiet guy, employable, came to the bar now and then, never said too much. Handsome too—looked like a billboard ad for plaid shirts. To Lester they had always seemed like deer together, graceful and quiet and attentive. At ease with each other.

"What's up?"

"I'm not what he thinks he's headed for."

"What do you mean?"

"He thinks he's bound to marry some six-foot tiny-assed blond woman who doesn't smoke, never loses her temper, and shaves her pubic hair."

"Who?"

"I don't know, he doesn't either, I don't think. But he keeps waiting and waiting. In the meantime he hangs out with me."

"What makes you think that's what he wants?"

"Don't be naive, Lester. That's what everyone wants."

"It isn't what *I* want."

"Of course it is."

"What's happened lately?"

"Nothing. Nothing has happened lately. We both go to work and eat breakfast and we play pool and go to movies. He pays off his truck loan. He likes me, feels comfortable around me, but wonders when his ship is going to come in. One of these days he'll win the lottery. He's optimistic like that. When I first met him it was part of what I liked."

"Does he say this, that he's waiting for someone better?"

"No, of course not."

"Then what makes you so sure that's what he thinks?"

"Sometimes you just know things, you know?"

The falls roared on and on. Lester didn't have any reply for that. He seemed to rarely just know things. He had been so astonished at Rhonda's departure that he wondered afterwards if he understood anything about her and what she had wanted. But Rhonda wasn't six feet tall and blond, and he wanted her. The only thing she was was gone. Cindee and Rhonda had become friends through Lester, and though he knew the women still spoke to one another, Cindee never talked with Lester about Rhonda. He had wanted a hundred times to ask her what she knew of Rhonda's reasons for leaving but had always bitten off the question. After a while he stopped always wanting to ask, but he still wondered why.

"Do you think anyone ever knows why anyone else loves you, or stops loving you?"

"Lester, it was good that she left. And it will be good when I get it together enough to leave Sam. Those two don't want us."

The Rushing River Falls were visible from nearly any-place in Rushing River township and audible anywhere out of doors; they were the whole reason for the town to exist. In the 1880s the falls had become a tourist des-tination, and the train was put through expressly to take advantage of the anticipated visitor traffic. Since then, representations of the town had been spread through the continent in a thousand glass bubbles of water and miniature snowy waterfalls and tiny perfect houses abut-ting the cataract. Even now the town could no more be thought of as existing independently of the falls than Banff could be thought of without mountains and lakes.

Or Wawa and its giant goose. Twenty-six feet, eighteen inches, total height.

The first man to attempt to ride over the falls did so in a rum barrel the day after Armistice Day, 1918. The barrel was shattered on the rocks and his pulped body was gathered up with dip nets in the pool below. After this there was a succession of attempts in steadily more elaborate vehicles—the first nonlethal ride was made by a twenty-two-year-old man named Roy Bodner in 1932 in a steel ball. He nearly asphyxiated, and spent the remainder of his years in the Rushing River Memorial Hospital drooling into a towel. He died in 1976, a local hero. Following his lead, there were episodic rides made throughout the forties and fifties, in balls and barrels of different designs. One man alone had made five success-ful trips over the falls, in a vehicle he called the *Roy Bodner*. In an effort to discourage these stunts the town council had passed an ordinance that dictated that sur-vivors of the trip would be fined ten thousand dollars upon their rescue. Making the trip illegal of course only made the undertaking more attractive to the folks who were drawn to such things anyway, and soon the river was filled with drifting and bobbing cylinders and spheres and pyramids with snorkels protruding. It wasn't until a hydro diversion upstream nearly doubled the water flow in the river that the problem abated. In one weekend in 1973, eight barrel riders disappeared. Concerned about the tourist traffic, the town rescinded the ordinance, but word was out: the falls were no longer passable, spoiled like so much of the country. Rushing River was nearly forgotten overnight.

The barrel riders had left their mark on the town, however, and even now were remembered in neon signs along Main Street, announcing perpetual vacancies to the world at the Splash 'n' Dash Motel and the price of grilled cheese sandwiches at the Foamy Water Café. The townspeople remembered, as well, the sight of the terrified young men and women as they walked up and down the sidewalks of Main Street the night before their attempt. The bartenders, at one time, were adept at judging how many hours the prospective rider had to wait from the rate at which their jauntiness eroded. Just pulled into town: swaggering and laughing. Six hours to go: lips pulled tightly back, eyes narrowed, disposed to vomiting. But the riders were all gone now and the town was the less for it. The floodlights danced against the falling water and it was still beautiful, but duller.

After many minutes of not talking, Lester and Cindee both stood up and walked back to the stairs down to the bar.

"Hey Lester?"

"Yeah?"

"Do you mind waiting until I get to the bottom before starting down?"

"No problem, Cindee."

"Thanks, Lester."

When they got back, Marilyn was in a white-hot burn. Harold's trousers bulged as if a trio of fattened ground squirrels had wedged themselves in there. The line of eager beer purchasers was twenty deep. Lester set to tending bar. Somebody was spraying beer into the mouth of somebody's girlfriend.

Cindee cashed out fifteen minutes after closing time and grabbed one of the cabs waiting outside beside the still-milling crowd. Ten minutes after that, Sam showed up. Lester was sweeping the floor and Marilyn was counting her money. She tipped out five dollars to Lester. Just to make herself clear. Sam knocked on the door and Lester let him in. He felt guilty, for knowing what was in store for Sam before Sam did, and he would not compound that by being rude to him.

Lester poured him a bourbon and Sam sat down at the bar. "Cindee's not around?"

"Just missed her. You want some chicken wings with that? They're still hot."

"Well, if they're still hot."

"Coming right up."

Lester brought a platter of wings the size of a garbage can lid and pulled up a stool opposite Sam at the bar. He opened a beer for himself. "How are you, Sam?"

"Fine as wine, Lester. Could use some more work these days, but otherwise I'm fine."

"What kind of work do you do again?"

"I'm a welder."

"What do you weld, Sam?"

"I can weld anything. Aluminum, stainless steel, titanium, magnesium, anything. Electric arc, tungsten inert gas, oxyacetylene, I do all those. Got my tickets for aeronautical work and pipelines. Since the Rockwell plant shut down, there's not much call for the fancy stuff anymore. I liked that work—delicate, precise joints in wild alloys. But even black iron is fun to me. Pulling the bead along a plate never gets old for me." Sam lifted his glass to that. Lester too.

"Sounds kind of stupid, making such a fuss about it like that, but it always gives me a charge. I think it's great work—making things out of parts."

"Sounds like it."

"You mean stupid or great?

"Oh no, great. Melting metal so that it is joined to another piece. Smoothly and evenly."

"Yeah. It is."

"You about done that bourbon?"

"Are you offering?"

"I'm offering."

"Then I'm accepting."

Lester refilled his glass.

"Cindee looked okay when she left, did she?"

"Sure. I guess she's been a little moody lately," Lester said.

"She's got a lot on her mind," Sam replied.

"I guess so."

"It eats at her."

"Nice woman, though."

Sam looked right at him. "Yes."

They went to work on the wings then. Lester ate four-fifths of them and even so Sam leaned back stuffed before Lester wiped the last of the sauce up with a bread roll. They drank their drinks, two men never previously alone with one another, full of barbecued chicken wings in the empty bar. The lights bounced off the heavy cigarette smoke that hung like fog. The cashout was done and the staff had scurried out, headed either for all-night restaurants or late-night television, and just like he always was, Lester was the last one there, nearly alone. Like always.

He stretched and turned around on his stool, away from the bar. "This is a stupid job for a man my age."

"You don't like it?"

"It's easy, but it's not, you know, not very beautiful. The way welding is, say. I never talk about bartending like that."

"Welding is the only thing I talk like that about."

"It's something."

"It is." They sat there another few minutes and then Sam started rubbing his eyes.

"I don't know how you guys manage to work in all this smoke. Hey, do you want to get out of here, go for a drive?"

"Sure."

And they got up and walked to the door. Lester stopped to turn on the alarm and lock up behind them. Then Lester got in his truck and Sam got in his. Sam pulled out and Lester followed him out to the lake road and into the industrial park. They pulled into one of the lots. Sam got out of his truck and unlocked a chain-link fence gate and opened it. They drove inside and Sam locked it behind them. Around them were stacks of old car wrecks, train axles, and farm machinery. Among and through this a path led to an old corroded Quonset hut that they could just make out in the moonlight. The two men walked there and Sam opened the door with a key. "I rent this place for a hundred bucks a month. It's where I spend most of my time these days." He reached inside and flipped a breaker switch.

Floodlights lit up a cone of night filled with twitching and flickering insects in the sky and spirals of twisted and deranged-looking steel on the ground. Around them, the shadows withdrew before dozens of shining and bent towers of steel and aluminum. There was a tyrannosaurus just a few feet from them, towering and menacing beside a stegosaurus in stainless steel, cringing on the oil-stained concrete floor. Lester gaped. In the last year of his life there had been no unexpected whimsy at all; even before that, stretching back years, he could not remember anything like this.

"Sam," Lester said, "this is just beautiful."

"Thanks. It's just busy work, stuff I do when I don't have enough to keep myself occupied."

Lester sat down on a sawhorse. He felt comparatively unambitious—all he had done in his spell of inactivity was eat. The stegosaurus with its twisted neck, looking up at the tyrannosaurus, had an obvious terror about it, a sense of immediate misery that Lester, for one, felt qualified to assess. It was deeply frightening.

"Who's going to win?" he asked, nodding at the creatures.

"I don't know. Depends on who's the most scared, or hungry, I guess."

"Looks like the tyrannosaurus is."

"I don't know. When I built them I thought that, too, but lately I've been looking at them and I think the stegosaurus might have a chance. Don't you think he looks like he has a trick or two left?"

"Maybe. That tail looks pretty formidable."

"Think about getting hit with that in the centre of the head."

"Just when you thought you had lunch all sewed up."

"Yep. You want to see something else?"

"Sure."

Sam walked to a tarp-covered mound in one corner of the shop and uncovered a silver cylinder, closed at one end, with a hatch screwed shut in the other. "Before I left Rockwell, the project we were all working on was an escape module for the submarines that they were going to propose to the navy, after that sub went down in the Bay of Fundy. She's half-inch stainless steel all around and was designed to be able to withstand the water pressure at ten thousand feet. The project was never that well thought out, though, and was cancelled when real paying work came our way."

Lester stared at the silver cylinder. "So this is it, this is the escape module?"

"Well, it was one of a bunch of prototypes."

"No kidding."

"When they told everyone that the contract was cancelled I was home with the flu. When I came in the next day the place was empty. I explained to the security guard that I had to pick up my tools and he just waved me in. When I was standing in the shop with everything lying where it had been dropped and nobody there, well, I just put the module on a ceiling hoist and put it in the back of my truck beside my tools and covered everything with that tarp.

"It's been here ever since, over ten years now. I've been thinking about what I could use it for."

"Not having a submarine of your own," Lester said.

"Yeah."

"Do you have any ideas?"

"I've been thinking that it would be a great barrel to ride over the falls in."

"Of course."

The next night after work, Lester drove to the Billy Burger Drive-Thru and then he drove off onto a side street to eat in his truck. He was listening to the all-night deejay talking about something to do with mad cow disease and the CIA when he saw Rhonda walking down the sidewalk with someone. He didn't recognize the man but he was tall and thin and had one arm around her. They walked like they were a little drunk. He watched them for a couple of blocks and then they turned and went into a townhouse. Lester didn't know if it was his place or her place or their place. He finished his Billy Burger and milkshake and onion rings and then he drove ahead. He looked in as he passed. There was a light on in the living room. There were car parts on the front lawn and the grass needed cutting. Lester kept driving and as he made his way back to his trailer his massive body shook. When he pulled up in his own debris-littered front yard he sat there and sobbed.

The next night after closing, Lester and Cindee sat at the bar, drinking. "Sam and I hung around the other night."

"He said as much."

"Are you still determined to move out?"

"I don't know. He pretends, but we lie about five feet apart in bed. Some days I feel up to just walking and other days I think, This is as good as anyone can realistically hope for. I'm not some model, I can't blame Sam for not seeing me as one."

"I don't have anything smart to say about that stuff."

"Me either."

"That's quite a shop he has out there."

"Did he show you his dinosaurs?"

"Yeah. I liked them."

"Did he tell you he thought you were a loser?"

"He seemed to me like a good guy."

She smoked her cigarette and patted him kindly on his massive arm.

That night after he locked up, Lester drove past the townhouse again. There were no lights on. He parked his truck down the street and then he sat down on the curb and watched the house. There was no movement. It was almost three in the morning. He picked up a pebble and threw it at one of the windows. There was no response. He picked up another pebble and threw it at the same window again. All quiet.

Lester walked back to his truck. He lowered the gate of the box and pulled out the object that was back there. He carried it to the townhouse, where he pushed the old manual lawn mower onto the grass and began cutting the lawn. It wasn't as noisy as a gas mower but in the still night the squeaking of the long-unused mower rang out as he pushed it back and forth on the front lawn. Lights flashed on up and down the street and Lester could see shadowy heads poking through windows. He ignored them. In the wet dew-laden grass, the mower did not cut well, and Lester had to redo many stretches, but after an hour he stood before the nicely trimmed lawn panting heavily, with sweat running down his face. Then a bright flashlight shined off of him like he was a jack-lit deer. At first the police officer did not know whether Lester was bawling or what.

"Lester, what the hell are you doing?" Jack Thompson asked.

"I'm cutting the grass."

"When did you move here, Lester?"

"I didn't. My wife did."

"Oh yeah. Been drinking, Lester?"

"A little."

"Did you drive here?"

"Maybe."

"Ah, Lester," Jack said, "now why are you getting mixed up in one of these situations? She's been gone what, a year? And you're pulling the crazed ex-husband thing now?"

"Eighteen months."

"I'd better drive you home."

"Okay."

The next night there were four fights in the lineup to get into the bar and the deejay played nothing but late-seventies disco for three hours, in a spasm of nostalgia for a better and hairier time. The kids thought it was great, the staff complained mightily, and only Lester was stirred nearly to tears, leaning against the bar and the mirror frame simultaneously and blinking.

Lester was thirty-six years old. When this music had come out he had been fifteen and thought it awful. He still did. Then he had been going to high school up in Dunsmuir like it was a conveyor belt, riding it there in the morning, through his classes, and then home. After he got out of the Air Force he moved to Rushing River, and worked for eight years in a plumbing supply warehouse. He played hockey in a no-contact league and spent more and more time at the Rushing River Bar and Grill after games. Everyone liked him there, he never got sloppy drunk, and when one of the bartenders got hurt in a car accident he was asked if he wanted some part-time work. He said yes and made more money in a weekend than he made in a week at the plumbing supply store and so he stayed at the bar.

He bought his trailer and met Rhonda; they went to movies on the weekends for a year and then she moved in. She wanted them to buy a house and they started saving for one. He had owned four automobiles in this time, and had had one DWI charge that had shook him up. No accidents, hadn't cheated on Rhonda, was losing a step in hockey. The last year he and Rhonda had sex less often but they didn't fight at all. Sometimes she wouldn't hear what he was saying and then would turn to him and without moving her eyes say, "Sorry, what was that?" And then she left and he had taken it a little hard. This was his life, since K.C. and the Sunshine Band had been on the charts. There was little that was remarkable here: without succeeding at anything conspicuously, he had managed to create a world that treated him gently for the most part and made him feel at home. And now, if he were trussed up and hanging naked on a hook in a meat freezer he couldn't have felt worse.

When Sam came in that night to pick up Cindee, Lester said to him, "I want to take that barrel over the falls."

Cindee had known Rhonda from before she and Lester started seeing each other. They had gone to school together but never in the same class. They had had ex-boyfriends and marginal friends in common. For a long time Cindee had not liked Rhonda much, had found her suspect, furtive almost. You saw it the clearest when she felt uncomfortable, at a party, say, when she couldn't remember somebody's name, and tried to hide it when it would have been easier to just get it out of the way. Or just in the way Rhonda had stayed in that little trailer out on the edge of town all by herself, even after she wasn't working anymore. Fear ran through that woman like a bad secret, Cindee thought, and you never knew how much she was holding back. It was that same quality that drew Lester in when they met, that startled and frightened look she had. Cindee watched it happen and smiled tightly and ached for Lester. Not that Rhonda wasn't entitled to leave Lester, or to have an unsuccessful marriage with him. But. When it seemed that inevitable, it ending so badly, it just made you wonder what they were thinking.

For people to be kind to each other shouldn't be the hardest thing in the world. Not to ask the world of each other, not to expect to be deliriously happy. Just to observe a few of the obvious rules, the ones that get broken so often. A certain amount of consideration. If you could have that it would be so much better than nothing.

Cindee didn't really give Rhonda a chance until many months after her and Lester's wedding. Cindee and Lester had always been work friends and Lester had suggested over and over again that she and Sam should come over for a barbecue or something. As eager as Lester was for all of them to be friends, Cindee couldn't shake her reservations about Rhonda. Finally she ran out of excuses and they all got together one night in July in Lester and Rhonda's backyard when the mosquitoes were like airborne pepper and the humidity was so high that everyone's crotch itched.

Lester and Sam had stood by the barbecue in floral-print shorts, mesmerized by the flames under the meat. Lester weighed maybe 140 pounds then. "Think we should turn it?" one would say to the other.

And the other would reply, "I dunno, maybe in a minute."

This left Cindee and Rhonda on the lawn chairs groping for conversation. "Do you remember any summers hotter than this?" Cindee asked.

"I don't think so," Rhonda replied. "How are the boys doing with the meat, do you think?"

Cindee shrugged and drank her piña colada.

"We've never used that barbecue before. Lester hates anything unfamiliar. I'm glad Sam is here to help him."

Cindee looked over at the two men, standing slack-jawed by the smoking barrel. She looked back at Rhonda and realized for an instant how frustrating it would be to live with Lester's passivity. As good a quality as it was, with all the hotheads around the bar, it would be hard, at night, or when the toilet started overflowing, or when you were trying to plan a vacation. She was glad Lester had met Rhonda, had found someone who loved him. Certainly it could have easily been her. Thank God it wasn't. "I'm glad you're around, to help Lester."

"He doesn't need that much help, actually. Just encouragement."

"Still," Cindee said.

Rhonda smiled. "He speaks highly of you, at the bar. He's very fond of you. When we first started seeing each other I thought maybe he was in love with you."

"That's *hilarious*."

"I know," Rhonda said. She sipped her drink and nodded at the mounting inferno. "Sam is quite a catch. Easygoing, competent, nice-looking."

"Thanks. I like him fine."

"Let's get the potato salad dished up."

Lester and Sam stared at the meat. "Do you think we should turn it?" Sam asked.

"I dunno, maybe in a minute," Lester said.

Cindee and Rhonda became friends more quickly than either woman expected. As they got to know one another better, Rhonda started to complain about Lester more and more. He was so perfunctory in bed, he was so emotionally remote, he never said what was really on his mind, only what he thought he had to say to reassure her. Cindee listened to this and had to acknowledge that she had seen all these things at work too, well, except the bed stuff, and she could see Rhonda's point. *Points*. There were a few of them.

But she wondered why Rhonda dwelled upon them. Lester wasn't going to change much. Shouldn't she get used to it? To him? And anyway, Cindee was Lester's friend too, she didn't necessarily want to hear about his sex life. But Rhonda was desperate for an ear, and there is something compelling about another woman being frank about her sex life, about how frustrating it is. Hearing you're not the only one.

And then Rhonda left Lester and everyone seemed so astonished and Cindee just wondered where everyone had been. He didn't make her happy and that point couldn't be argued. But there was the question of whether or not he should have made her happy—which nobody ever wants to talk about: as if people have no control over their feelings, you feel what you feel is all, like we are all sea anemones, tasting the water and filtering whatever comes our way. But she *should* have been happy with him—Cindee was prepared to say this.

In the end it was inevitable that she would leave, and that was hardly a bad thing, if she was determined to be that unhappy with him. Except when you looked at poor Lester, who was poleaxed. But that capacity for sorrow was in him before he met Rhonda. Cindee knew that. Oh, Cindee didn't know what to think.

What had Rhonda seen when she looked at herself in the mirror that she would be so unsatisfied with Lester? What's not to be happy with? Idiot. Don't stare too hard at someone else's cellulite unless you can stand in front of the mirror and look at your own little bulges just as hard. Who does she think she is, Miss America? Why can't we be happy with one another, anyway?

The barrel was basically ready to go from a structural point of view. It had been designed to survive a drop farther than the height of the falls, and into deep water too. There was good flotation present and brackets for oxygen tanks. As a welder, Sam had lots of oxygen tanks lying around, so that wasn't a problem, but there was a question of how best to regulate the oxygen flow. This wasn't really Sam's field. The other thing was, once the barrel was shut up tight, where would the carbon dioxide go—and what sort of flow rate should the oxygen have, and how do you keep that constant with no vent and a steadily increasing pressure inside the barrel? Unless you did put a vent in. But then that meant a hole in the barrel. Lester wasn't much use on any of these questions, but he came by every night after work with beer and wings anyway, to chat, to hold things.

Sam looked at Lester sometimes, and tried to figure out why he was doing this. He knew a little bit about the trouble he'd had for the last year, and all that weight he had put on, of course that was obvious. But who knows what makes anyone else tick? Not Sam.

Sam was the best welder Sam had ever known. This was simply a fact. At the Rockwell plant he was considered a prodigy; all the engineers asked for him to work on their prototypes. It had been great then, working around people who cared as much as he did about flaw-less work and craftsmanship and could appreciate the attention he put into it. Since then it had been hard, being another out-of-work guy. It's hard to not want to be the best and to be seen that way. Which sounds ungracious to say out loud, but doesn't anyone who tries hard think like that? As opposed to people who have given up, say. You don't want to be like that. It's dangerous even to pretend to be all modest and helpless like that. It really is.

All around Sam were people who were just coasting, just trying to get used to their shitty jobs and their

marginal marriages. Cindee and Lester and the losers
they worked with down at that bar—look at their days.
Sleep till noon or one o'clock, get up and eat cereal and
smoke cigarettes in front of the television. Get dressed in
the mid-afternoon. Maybe run an errand, do a crossword
puzzle, and then go to work. Home at three or four. Fall
asleep as the sun rises. Just what are you going to accom-
plish living like that? These people hate themselves and
they reveal this in every faked and hearty laugh and in
every round they buy for their friends, after closing, in
that dark and stinking-of-cigarette-smoke bar.

You have to aim for something bigger, just to stand
yourself. Anything will do, almost. Anything even a little
out of reach is worthwhile. You have to choose a beautiful thing, imagine better, or everything around you just
gets worse.


It was dawn and Cindee and Sam and Lester were at the
lookout over the falls. Lester and Cindee were sitting on
the fenders of Sam's truck. The light was stabbing silver
and bright through the mist below the falls. Sam was
standing on the safety rail, balancing easily and looking
down. Lester and Cindee drank from bottles of beer
they cradled in their laps. Lester was nervous about Sam
falling over. Cindee told him not to worry.

"We've been coming down here a couple times a
month as long as we've known each other. He always
does this. At first I thought he was trying to impress me

and I thought it was sort of stupid and sort of cute." She said that loudly enough for Sam to hear and Sam looked over his shoulder at them and smiled quickly. Then, more quietly: "But then I realized that, like with everything, he's just trying to impress himself."

"Reassure himself, maybe."

"Maybe."

Another crazy-busy summer night after closing, after rousing the unconscious and herding them to the door and pushing them into cabs and then collapsing likewise into the chairs around the bar and not talking much, just rubbing your temples. Cindee and Marilyn and Lester were drinking their first beers of the night when Sam knocked on the door. No one moved for a long moment. Finally Cindee put her cigarette in an ashtray and stood up and walked over to the door and opened it and walked back to her chair. Sam followed her, waving his hand in front of his face. "It reeks in here," he said.

Cindee exhaled slowly. "It was nuts tonight."

"You all look terrible."

"Well, we're tired."

"Then maybe you don't need more to drink."

Cindee looked up at him. "Does this disgust you, Sam? Do I disgust you, Mr. Chiselled Jaw?"

Lester crossed his legs and stared at a wall. Marilyn looked up at Sam with detached disdain. Sam turned and walked out the door.

The tradition had always been to launch barrels very early on Sunday mornings, when the police were sleeping. Lester and Sam had spent Saturday afternoon going over the barrel one more time. They had double-checked all the safety systems—the air bags inside the barrel, the breathing apparatus and the backup oxygen supply, the radio. It all worked perfectly. That night Cindee and Lester worked at the bar, and, through all the smoke and music, Lester had felt as if he were stoned, moving slowly and easily through the line of customers, all urgently twitching to the music and looking impatiently at the repulsive and obese bartender who seemed hardly to hear them as they shouted out for their brands of beer and tequila.

Cindee stared at Lester all night long, and was likewise a target of abuse from the college kids. As she held her tray high and pushed along, the crowd would part and at the other end of the room she could see Lester there, rubbing his chin and smiling and blinking.

When she walked up to the bar, Lester didn't recognize Rhonda at first, but turned and asked her what she wanted, prepared to reach for one of the beers, and then looked up at her non-response and it was her. "Hi," he said.

"Lester, I've heard about this barrel ride you're planning and I came by to tell you that I think this is even more pathetic than that business on Jerry's lawn."

"Oh," Lester said.

"So don't do this, and spare us both the humiliation, okay?"

"What do you mean?"

"Don't embarrass me, don't embarrass yourself."

"Why would either of us be humiliated?"

"Lester, please tell me you won't do this."

"Okay."

"Thank God." They exchanged a long look and then Rhonda turned and walked away.

Cindee stopped by the bar and looked at Lester. He seemed to be moving even more slowly. "How are you, Lester?"

"I'm excited," he said. He didn't look it.

"What did Rhonda want?" Cindee asked.

"To wish us luck."

"Really?"

"Yep."

Cindee didn't sleep at all that night. Sam stayed down at his shop, tinkering with the barrel as Cindee sat on the edge of their bed. Sam and Lester were both idiots. Neither one of them could get used to his own life. Lester, in his pout, which looked to be becoming permanent, and Sam and his wouldn't-belong-to-any-club-that-would-take-me ambition. The other night he had told her that anything a little out of reach was a worthwhile goal. Like anyone around him is not?

She lit another cigarette and flipped the ash into a coffee cup. She looked at herself in the mirror, her tear-streaked face and her breasts, hanging down, her arms, reaching around and hugging herself.

In the morning Lester sat out on his porch waiting for Cindee to come by. When she pulled up in Sam's truck Lester stood and waved to her. She got out of the truck and walked up to him. "Having any second thoughts?" she said.

"None worth mentioning," he said.

"Are you still excited?"

"Not as much. It's all afterthought now. How are you doing?"

"Better, thanks."

"Good. I don't know if Sam thanked you for us, but I really appreciate your help here."

"Lester, I'm only helping out because you're involved."

"How's Sam?"

"He's fine. He thinks he's gonna be famous."

"Do you think we will?"

"Depends if anyone sees us, I guess." And they got into Sam's truck and drove over to the shop, where he had been up all night, double-checking.

When they got the barrel to the river upstream of the falls it was already very light and the streets were starting to wake up. Fishermen began appearing on the river, and the last of the morning mist dissipated. Lester climbed into the back of the truck. Sam swung the hatch of the barrel open and Lester squeezed himself in feet first. He buckled up the elaborate harness. For the first time he began to feel afraid. He looked up out the hatch and saw Cindee and Sam looking in. Cindee was almost crying and Sam looked stern, even angry.

"Are you okay?" Cindee asked.

"No," Lester said.

"What's the matter?" Sam asked. Lester didn't reply. He shut his eyes tightly and swallowed repeatedly. Lester felt ridiculous and pathetic, a fat helpless man in a barrel, like a giant fish being transported by a zoo.

"Look, are you going to go through with this or not?" Sam asked. "Because if you won't, I will."

"What's the matter?" Cindee repeated.

"I just have to adjust the harness," Lester said. "I just need a minute." He almost said he didn't want to do it but then the familiar feeling of acquiescent helplessness swept through him and he thought that none of this mattered at all, he didn't matter at all. Look at the last year of his life. "Okay," he said, leaning his head back against the wall of the barrel. "Let's go."

"Okay," Sam said. And he closed the hatch and locked it. Lester put the oxygen regulator into his mouth. Sam knocked on the barrel and Lester knocked back twice, their signal to go ahead. Lester heard them clamping the steel ramp to the back of the truck and then the barrel began rolling onto the ramp and then quickly down and into the water.

He heard the water splashing around the barrel and it felt to him like he wasn't moving but rather just bobbing up and down. He pressed the transmit button on the radio. "Guys, it feels like I'm hung up on something here, some bushes or something."

Sam's voice crackled back to him, "No, I've got you in sight, you're in the current now and moving pretty quickly."

"Are you sure? It doesn't feel like it."

"Yes, I'm sure. Remember what we said about staying loose."

"Yeah."

"We're in the truck now and driving alongside the river. Jesus, you're going fast. We're going to run ahead now to get the boat into the water, so we might be out of range for a few minutes, but we'll be waiting for you beneath the falls."

"Uh, okay."

"Just a second . . ." There was a pause. Cindee's voice came over the radio.

"Lester, everything is going to be okay, you know that, don't you?"

"Yeah, Cindee, I do."

"Good."

"See you at the bottom," Lester said. There was no reply. Probably the truck had already sped up, out of range.

What Lester hadn't anticipated was how little there was to do. He couldn't see out of his barrel, he had no idea how far he was from the falls, and it didn't really matter anyway because here he was trussed up and unable to steer or do anything except wait for a sense of falling. His only contribution to this undertaking was to sit in this barrel and feel terrified. Just sit still and *feel*. Powerless and immobile.

The barrel should have had a rudder of some sort, some way that the barrel could be steered. He could have insisted on that. And a little window that he could look out of. If it had just those things then this would not be quite as preposterous a thing to be doing.

The barrel began slowly rotating. This was Lester's first clue that he was entering the turbulent area above the falls. He didn't know how long it would take now, and then the barrel began bucking up and down like a mechanical bull and then abruptly it stopped.

Cindee and Sam were already in the pool beneath the falls, in the Boston Whaler that Sam had rented. The barrel appeared as a tiny black dot far above them and they both sucked their breath in when they saw it. It hung for an instant at the lip of the falls and then it was in mid-air and it fell. Like it weighed four thousand pounds. They both watched it closely through binoculars right up until the barrel disappeared in the foam. It was unexpectedly tiny-looking in the great plumes of water. Studying the bottom of the falls, they saw only water bouncing up and around more water, and there were no silver floating cylinders anywhere at all.

"Do you see it?" Sam called out.

"No, do you?" Cindee answered. They both searched the pool beneath the falls frantically. Both felt as though they couldn't breathe. Over and over again they motored as close as they could to the whirlpool at the bottom of the falls and peered into the curtain of water and saw nothing at all. "Jesus Christ," Sam said. They drove back and forth and around and around and did not speak to each other. They hung their heads over the gunwales of the boat until they were nearly underwater and the waves rose up and broke over them and Cindee and Sam were wiping water from their eyes. It seemed to Cindee that this could not be happening, but she had thought that about different things and of course it could be, and it was.

After two hours they gave up and motored back to shore to call the police. They climbed the stairs that led to the observation point. There was a pay phone there. They stopped and looked back at the water swirling around and around and not expelling Lester or the barrel.

"What do you think happened?" Cindee asked.

"I don't know. Maybe it fell too deep and hit bottom. I didn't really take into account how fat he was."

By this point Lester's barrel was already five miles down-river, fetching up on a sandbar, and jerking to a halt. Blood oozed from Lester's ears and ran over his face from the pressure of the air bags exploding and he could not see to turn on the radio. But he could reach the lock of the hatch, and when it fell open the barrel only half filled with water.

Cindee and Sam walked to the pay phone beside the rail. They stopped as Sam felt his pockets for a quarter. "You are such a sonofabitch," Cindee said.

Sam turned his back on her and looked out at the water. He thought he saw something, and pointed. Cindee leaned forward over the rail. Sam climbed the rail and stood on it, shading his eyes and staring. Nothing. Just water glinting in the sun. Cindee reached over and pushed behind Sam's knees. He looked down wildly, as he toppled. Sam grabbed for the rail as he fell but he had too much momentum to stop himself and he swept by, his chin hitting the lip of concrete beneath the rail. She watched as he hit the water, making a huge splash. She thought she saw his face staring upward for an instant and then he disappeared in the current.

Cindee wondered again that that could have just happened, but it had. She stood clutching the rail and stared at the water and the falls and all that mist. Then she walked back to the pay phone to call 911 and report another drowning beneath the falls.

Lester pulled himself out and stood heaving and shivering on the riverbank. Every time he shivered his flesh rippled like a waterbed through his wet T-shirt. He wiped the blood from his face and pushed the barrel back into the current and watched it float away, filling with water through the open hatch. He lay back on the riverbank and looked at the sky.

This was in 1997.

When Cindee and Sam had first met they were very young and not conscious of their beauty. In those days she was disconcerted by admiration, found it suspect and threatening. In large groups—at church, for instance, when they both still went—they drew glances from everyone. It would not last. They knew that even then. The attention was not a function of their substance, she thought, and was meaningless. But she was wrong. Beauty is of the essence, is evidence of what lies beneath, and it bleeds into what lies beneath: either way, the beautiful are or become a certain way. They feel and think and act like beautiful people. They can easily be identified even by the blind, or over the telephone.

Later, after he was dead, she remembered what he had looked like, what she had looked like, in various mirrors in motel rooms and apartments around the prairie. She recalled sitting astride him and staring at his neck, taut, like cable under load. She recalled watching him watch her in the ugly large and plastic-framed mirror in that furnished apartment they had rented. The rural Manitoba rental market being what it is, there wasn't often much beauty in the linoleum and wood-panelled rooms they had lived in. But they could have sold tickets to the sight of them dressing in the morning.

# INTERPOSITION

In her neighbourhood she was as much a fixture as the *caserne de pompiers*; when she'd walk to a café, barks and whistles followed her like she was the sausage truck. Her daughter was nine years old and had thick black hair and long limbs like a marionette; on the street mother and child were constantly assailed by old women and street cleaners with their respective exclamations of approval. Mother and daughter bore these nuisances with equal equanimity and perfect poise. The child's name was Giselle and she understood very well why she was fussed over.

The child's father was Leonard, an engineer who had studied at MIT and then returned home to France with his American girlfriend in tow. It's okay, my family will adore you and even if things are a little cool right at first, who cares, let's just have some fun and enjoy ourselves.

Which is the sort of thing young men are prone to saying, for the first six months.

Paris is expensive, there is no escaping this. Tourists shake their heads at the ten-dollar sandwiches and just sort of assume that there is a secret menu for the locals, one that more closely approximates the Piggly Wiggly experience. But there isn't, Paris is obscene, that's all. And the French acknowledge this, once they've established that there are no social points to be made in impressing you. But, for them, Paris is also the only real city in the world, the only city that, in the end, isn't provincial, and so the four-dollar cups of coffee are conceded as sort of a poll tax on sophistication—they go with the territory, but just look at the territory, will you? And they have a point.

To American art students who didn't quite finish and now find themselves reading baby formula preparation instructions with a dictionary in hand, the poll tax seems a little more outrageous, and if the baby's father wants her to live in this city, then she's going to need a little more than five thousand lousy francs a month. Which, it seems, his family understands and so despite him, they reply with remarkable generosity and a matter-of-factness that shuts her up completely. Good Lord, must be some plumbing business.

Which brings her to the point of sitting in an old church by herself, listening to a harpsichord concert and wondering if people can tell just by looking at her how

ignorant she is. Even her daughter had heard of this guy
and had seemed to understand what the big deal is.

And when I made a face at the pompous introductions
she saw me and laughed. At the intermission she sidled
up beside me, drink in hand, hat firmly in place, and
said, in English, "Nice tapestries, huh?"

I said, "Is it that obvious?" And she nodded.

"The clothes," she said. I looked down at them,
unaware that the Gap had been betraying me.

"Is there no hope at all?"

"Wear primary colours only as a last resort and even
then as a gesture of self-parody."

"Maybe I should just go back home now."

"Had you been planning on being around for a
while?" she asked.

"My name is Robert."

Her child flirted with me outrageously on our first
meeting. Her eyes between her fingers, beside me on the
couch, she laughed like a bebop jazz trumpeter, all unin-
hibited flights of exuberance. "This will last until she
decides that you are a threat to her father," her mother
said. She waited for a response. I played some more with
the child. "Which I am very careful about," she added.

A month later: rising at four in the morning to sneak
out before Giselle awoke, walking down rue St. André
des Arts, the street cleaners soaking down the sidewalks,

which glisten like sweaty skin, our skin perhaps, a half hour previously. In midsummer in Paris the streets are the most comfortable place to spend the close, thick nights, and I did not hurry home. In Place St. Michel you can always get a croissant and *café crème* and so I stopped there to sit among drunken Scandinavians and derelicts and wait for the morning newspapers to be dropped off.

As I sat there, nursing my four-dollar cup of coffee, I thought of Leonard. He and I had not met but no day passed without a dozen references to him, by Giselle and her mother. It had been Leonard who had broken things off initially, before they had learned of the pregnancy. But he had adjusted more quickly to the prospect of being a father than he had to that of being a husband and before she knew it he had found her an apartment on rue de l'Éperon, two bedrooms, maybe five minutes from Place St. Michel, and he was there for the child's birth and for another couple of months following, fixing meals, washing diapers, buying groceries. And she appreciated this help, she said, but after a while she was wondering how long he intended to stay—the apartment was in his name, incidentally—and eventually she had to ask him to leave.

Which he had done. But he still saw his daughter every few days and most weekends, and when Giselle spoke of her grandparents it was only his mother and father she meant and she loved him dearly and spoke often of how much she liked it when he spent the night.

As far as the child went, my periodic presence in the apartment was a matter to be approached with tremendous care. Leonard knew of my existence long before Giselle was allowed to see me kiss her mother. I recall taking Giselle to her little school at the end of the street some months after our first meeting—I'd been kicked out for an hour, to stand in a morning downpour underneath the awning in the courtyard, in order to return as Giselle was eating her cereal—she held my hand as we walked down the street and she sang a children's song I didn't recognize, in French. Her friends ran up to greet her and she let go my hand and went running to them without a word. I watched her run all the way down the street to the school. The parents of the other children were kissing them and patting down their hair as they squirmed. The parents nodded *bonjour* to me. I nodded back and watched to see if the child got in okay, to wave to her. She ran straight up the steps, lifting her knees high, like she was running through mud. Her eyes might have wavered five degrees from the door just as she disappeared. I turned to go back to her mother.

Eventually Leonard asked to meet me in one of those American bars on the right bank, in the Marais. This, I suppose, was a gesture of some sort. He was there already waiting for me and I was fifteen minutes early. He ordered whiskeys without asking.

"I loved the States when I was there," he said, sitting back down after we shook hands. "I guess she told you, I did my degree at MIT." I nodded, smiling like a fool and taking a sip of my whiskey.

"I would have stayed but for my family, I guess. And visas were a headache in those days. Plus, she wanted to live in France."

Her account had been pretty different.

"So, I wanted to meet you," he said, and took a big gulp of his whiskey, looking past me, into the mirror behind the bar. He swallowed heavily and set his glass on the bar. "Because I thought it was about time we got together and talked about arrangements."

"Why didn't you want her to know that we were going to meet?" I asked.

"Well, you know, these things get so much more difficult if we start mixing broken hearts into all this."

As I recounted this conversation to her that night, sitting on the Quai aux Fleurs, she laughed like an idiot, on and on: "Oh God, how foolish he can be! He's not really so serious as he must have sounded, you know. I suppose he thought he was being adult." She handed me the wine bottle and I tipped it to my lips. Her friend Carol, from art school, was minding Giselle, a favour they exchanged often. We had another hour.

He went on: "I guess what we should talk about is what you intend to make in the way of a commitment. I think that it should be easy to understand that I'm not prepared to keep paying the apartment rent if you are going to live there more or less permanently."

"Sure."

"So what sort of a commitment, exactly, are you making?"

"Uh, you know, she and I haven't even had this conversation yet, I don't know what answer I have for you. I don't know what I'm going to do after my fellowship runs out. For the time being, I'm keeping my little apartment over in the seventeenth. I think that right now, we're letting the relationship define itself."

"That means nothing."

I sat back in my stool and held my shoulders a little straighter. "If you say so," I said.

"I say so."

And it went from there.

I handed her back the wine bottle. "Basically, he told me that I was an irresponsible trifler who was toying with your affections, not that it was any business of his, but also with the affections of his daughter, and he would not allow her to be hurt and that I had better be aware of that. He knew what I was up to, he said."

She stopped laughing. "I don't need him to watch out for Giselle."

"Still, I guess you can understand why he's concerned."

"Why?" she said.

"Uh, just that she's, you know, his daughter, and he doesn't know who I am or how long I'll be here. You know."

"Do both of you think I haven't considered this?"

"Of course you have."

"I can take care of us."

"I can't let you do that, we've talked about this."

"I didn't mean you." She was looking at me just like her husband had.

In the Luxembourg Gardens the child and I ate *croque monsieur* and discussed the strategy of the pitchout. Her mother was off negotiating. "Basically it boils down to intuition and good communication between the catcher, the pitcher, and the first and second basemen," I said.

"But most of the time you're going to end up giving away a free ball," she replied, peering across the metal table at me, squinting with the effort of trying to grasp the concept.

"Which is another reason why staying ahead in the count is so important, because of the options it gives you. And after it has worked once, for the rest of the game, the other team's baserunners take an extra look before heading for second."

"So it's the fact that you might use the play that matters more than using it." Swinging her skinny legs under her chair, her pleated plaid skirt tucked carefully under her, not a stray crease anywhere.

"You've just summarized baseball strategy."

"Will you take me to a Yankees game the next time we're back in the States?"

"Of course."

"When will that be, do you think?" Eyes like a hunting cat's. Not even the suggestion of a blink.

Waiting for her after her soccer game: I had cheered my lungs out, embarrassing her mightily but no more than I had irritated the *grande dame* beside me, who had cast her mean little eyes back and forth between me and the game with a *froideur* that could freeze your heart, but it was my throat that was weak and hoarse now and the child insisted on taking me for a *limonade* on our way home.

Setting down the glasses on our little round table she asked me if I had made a decision about what I was going to do in the fall. "Not yet," I said.

"Papa asks me that every time he talks to me." We both nodded at that.

"It's hard, figuring out what you can and can't do without sometimes."

She sipped her *limonade*, looking over her glass at me, sitting perfectly straight like no North American child not in a neck brace, and she set down the glass on the metal table and folded her hands in her lap. There was a long pause.

"Your mother will be wondering where we are."

"Yes," she said.

"We should go."

"Yes," she said.

I walked up the stairs to Leonard's apartment building. I was nauseous. It was after nine and she hadn't called. I had picked up the telephone four times before I decided to go over myself. Giselle had watched me leave the apartment from around the substantial waist of her Yugoslavian neighbour/landlady. Giselle didn't say anything, she just nodded at me when I said that I wouldn't be very long.

No answer at the heavy wooden door for a long time. And then Leonard answers, smiling and shrugging his bare shoulders. Come on in, a trace of apology at the indelicacy of the circumstances. I speak to her from the hall, standing there in my jacket. Her voice rolls around the corner, slow and guarded. He reappears in a shirt.

"So Maria will look after her for an hour or so but I said I wouldn't be any longer than that. You might want to hurry," I call to her around the corner.

"I was going to talk to you about this. It seemed clear to me what you wanted most," she said.

"Yes," I said.

"No hard feelings," Leonard says from the kitchen.

When I was packing up my apartment, a mutual friend came by with a parcel. It contained two shirts I had left at her apartment. No letter. The shirts smelled like Giselle and her mother and the smell of cooking food that seeped up from the floorboards. I was gone before the cold weather came.

This was in 1992.

Cindee quit her job at the bar and announced that she was moving back out west, to Brandon, where she would study cosmetology.

She and Lester wrote to one another frequently. She found a job that she liked, Lester learned, and she was pleased that she didn't have to work nights anymore. In the ensuing years they rarely alluded to the barrel ride, but notwithstanding the troubles the couple had had beforehand, Lester understood Sam's death to have been Cindee's great tragedy, her defining event.

He came to reconsider this point after she called him once late at night, drunk and angry with her current boyfriend. She was sputtering over his many shortcomings when Lester asked if any man for her would ever live up to the one she had lost. She laughed like an accordion, staccato wheezing into the telephone. He had no idea what to make of it.

Still later they met in Winnipeg, where they were both doing Christmas shopping. They ate supper together in a restaurant that revolved on top of a tower. It was very expensive but the food was quite carefully prepared. They were older and less nervous and sad than they had been. Cindee had moved on from that boyfriend, she said, still sorry about the phone call. They sat until long after the kitchen had closed. When they finally got up from their table, they had to be escorted through security. Outside they hesitated, but then caught separate taxis. Riding home, each thought about the Rushing River Waterfall and that long plunge.

# GABRIELLA:
## PARTS ONE AND TWO

### Gabriella (1)

Gabriella is an even six feet tall, has a nose that could split pack ice, and yearns constantly for her brother Hector. Hector is in the Argentine army, doing his obligatory service on a razor-wire-bordered base near the coast of Patagonia. Gabriella and her mother worry constantly about his catching cold; nineteen years old and surrounded by veterans of the Malvinas war, no doubt he appreciates their concern. It is on the matter of Hector only that Gabriella permits herself sentimentality—on all other topics she affects the cynicism of a big-city cop. When she speaks she leans forward, to put shoulder behind her words. She smokes foul-smelling South American cigarettes and tells bawdy jokes when she drinks pastis. She maybe drinks too much pastis.

Felicinada is only slightly shorter but much better humoured than Gabriella. She dresses always in yellow and has the largest collection of Xavier Cugat records in the world. When I had chicken pox last year she made me tomato soup every day for a week. They both work around the corner at the Café Kiev. They live above me and make an astonishing amount of noise. Felicinada, I think, wears high heels from the moment she gets up to when she goes to bed again. They are given to vacuuming at three in the morning, and inevitably they are *aficionadas* of the rumba. You can imagine.

" 'So look here, my little *machito*,' I says to him, 'you ask me for a Caesar salad. I bring you a Caesar salad. And now you won't pay for it because I didn't tell you it had anchovies in it. *Caesar salads have anchovies in them.* I'm sorry if you're lacto-ovulating these days but you still ordered the such-and-such salad and you're gonna pay for it.' " This is Gabriella. It is two in the afternoon and she is sitting on my couch and reading a fashion magazine. I can just see her through the crack in the bathroom door. Neither of us has seen Felicinada for three days. She has taken a lover and Gabriella is feeling a little abandoned. I can smell coffee brewing. I am in the tub, enveloped in bubbles.

I met Gabriella the week I moved into this apartment. The first night I slept here I awoke at four in the morning to the sound of running water coming from my bathroom. I sat up among the pillars of cartons all around me and listened. There was water splashing and there was humming. I paused outside the door and then edged it open slowly. "What sort of apartment is this," I remember wondering, in awe, "that comes with coffee-skinned amazons who bathe in your bathtub in the early morning?" And then our eyes met and we shrieked; she, rising up in the water and grabbing a back brush—*my* back brush—to serve as a club; me, slamming the door and leaping back. Through the suddenly latched, bolted, and leaned-against door, we established that she lived above me but that she didn't have a bathtub, only a shower, and that she had come to an agreement with her friend Susan, who had lived here before me and who worked nights, that she could use the tub anytime she wished before 8 a.m.; she hadn't realized Susan had left.

I, ever the agreeable one, suggested she carry on as she had with Susan. She snorted loudly at that. But she finished her bath and left with a nod. A month would pass—of observation? assessment?—before I would hear splashing in the night again and soon we were friends.

"Robert, your toast is getting cold," she calls. "You'll turn into a little squid if you don't hurry up."

She has croissants from the bakery, grapefruit juice, the toast and cereal with fresh fruit waiting—clearly an observer of the Most Important Meal dictum. She pours me coffee as I sit down. "Gabriella, this is great."

"Eat your food before it gets cold."

"Mmmmmggruph."

"Charlie has been getting worse lately," she says absently, as she picks up her magazine again. Charlie is the building superintendent. He lives across the hall from me, is married to a woman we all call Saint Dorothy, and wears silk suits and shoes that gleam like good intentions. He plays the cornet, or did once, and sometimes you can hear "Moon River" drifting through the hallways with the visceral poignancy of late-night television and too many mai tais. This despite the fact that when sober he prosecutes the noise-abatement bylaws like his personal *jihad*.

"Worse how?"

"Last night I'm just getting ready to go to work and he knocks on the door and he wants to know if the apartment needs any domestic maintenance to be done. That's what he said, 'domestic maintenance.' I said, 'It looks to me like you're more dressed to go meringue the night away than you are to be fixin' taps.' He bows to me and offers his arm and says, 'Whatever señorita wishes.' 'Charlie,' I say, 'I'd rather stick needles in my eyes than go dancing wit' you.' He says, 'Hard to get—that's a Latin thing, isn't it?'"

"Leapin' lizards."

"Men are beasts. All except my brother, Hector."

This is Gabriella's construct of the world: at the centre lies Hector, herself, and, when she's not off with some new dalliance, Felicinada. This is the limit of presumed good. In successive layers outward lie Carmen Miranda films, expensive outerwear, and her pastis. After that, pretty much everything is at least suspect. Way out in the stratosphere, even beyond her job at the Café Kiev and dental work, are men who use hair care products, stand too close, and never stop smiling even when they speak.

The front door swings open. In walk the prodigal roommate and a man who wears a torn and spattered tuxedo. "Hi guys," Felicinada says, then, nodding at the man in the mayonnaise stains, "this is Peter, he missed his train. He came up here last week for his cousin's wedding and we've been hanging around ever since." Peter is maybe twenty-eight. Peter is ignored. Gabriella continues reading her fashion magazine. Pointedly.

"Hi, Gabriella," Felicinada ventures. Something is said quickly in Spanish, in reply. There is a pause. Felicinada tightens her lips.

"Nice to meet you, Peter," I say.

Felicinada smiles at me and leads Peter away from the door. "How are things?" she says to me. Peter takes up a station beside the window, hands stuck deep in his tuxedo trousers. Felicinada sits down on the couch beside Gabriella, facing me.

"Awake till dawn again."

With a laugh and a leap in register, she says, "Us too." Gabriella's eyes make a slow, lazy loop-the-loop. The fashion magazine stays where it is. Peter's chin tilts toward his chest. He's wishing he were elsewhere.

"The week started off with a dinner dance?" I say to Peter.

"As far as I remember," he says, grinning widely, shrugging. He's not a bad guy, you can tell.

For Gabriella every expression of Felicinada's sexuality is a betrayal of their relationship. Gabriella's sense of self-denial is so strongly developed as to extend even to those around her. Peter clearly has no inkling of the titanic struggle being waged over him. I am not without pity, or envy.

Peter is talking about his job, which he is certain he has lost by now. Something to do with bondage. Or bonds, maybe he was making a joke.

"What are you going to do now?" I ask.

Felicinada is silent and pretends to be listening to Peter.

"Watch music videos until my attention span is the same duration as a sneeze," he says.

Gabriella. Reads. Her. Magazine.

From across the hall the sounds of Charlie warming up his horn drift through the walls. Afternoon practice. He starts up on "My Funny Valentine." "What in God's name is that?" asks Peter.

"Frustrated ambition," I say.

"A frustrated cock," Gabriella says, through her magazine.

"Is everyone crazy here?" Peter asks. And Charlie wails some more. A quiet knock on the door. I get up and open it, Dorothy's there, smiling. Come in, Dorothy, are you sure, sorry to be bothering, no bother, want some coffee, a croissant? It's just that it was getting a little loud and I could feel one of my headaches coming on. Jam or marmalade? You're such a dear.

Dorothy is in her early fifties and maintains her hair in a state of complete subjugation. She is always pleasant and wears aprons that she embroiders herself. I have no idea why she stays with Charlie. Gabriella thinks it has something to do with that hair.

"Good afternoon, my name is Peter and I'm from New York," Peter says.

"And what do you do in New York, Peter?"

"I am newly unemployed."

"Sorry to hear it, what are your plans?"

"I've just been thinking about that and I figure my severance pay would get me as far as Mexico City anyway."

"I hear Mexico City is lovely this time of year," Dorothy replies. Peter is looking at Felicinada, who is looking at the floor.

"Dorothy, you have to do something about Charlie— this is ridiculous," Gabriella snaps. With that, Charlie leaps into the break and the music fills the room, pure pathos and heartbreak.

"I know, dear, I tried to talk to him earlier today."

Felicinada, to Peter: "How long would you be going for?"

Gabriella, to me: "I don't know why we stand it, we pay rent here after all."

"I dunno. A couple months?"

Dorothy, to Felicinada: "Would you pass the creamer please, dear?"

Charlie launches into "A Night in Tunisia" and oh my God, I've never heard him play like this before, even through two doors and the hallway, no drunk plays like this. I look over at Dorothy, who is stirring her coffee. "Is this jam homemade?" she asks, pointing to her croissant. "I'd die for the recipe."

Felicinada says, "How would you be going?"

Peter says, "I have a VW Microbus that I keep out at my parents' in Yonkers. I was thinking I could drive it down."

Gabriella, facing me: "You can't ever make someone else responsible for your happiness. That's the first rule of sanity."

"Boy, that sounds like fun."

"Because the second you do that, and they see it, they have no choice but to let you down."

"Want some company?"

"Sure."

I listen to this music now and I am gooseflesh. Why haven't I heard him like this before? "Dorothy," I say, "what's with Charlie today?"

"I'm sorry, I know he must get on your nerves."

"No, not that, why is he playing like that?"

"Like what, dear?"

"All I need is about twenty minutes to pack."

"Are you sure?"

"Is this tea Earl Grey?"

"Sure I'm sure, c'mon, all I need is a raincoat and my toothbrush."

"He used to play like that all the time," she said, picking up Gabriella's magazine and looking at the front cover. "You think he's hard to take *now*."

*"You can't count on him."*

And the door squeaks open. Peter lifts his eyebrows and smiles as he is pulled upstairs. And then the door clicks shut.

Dorothy looks down at her magazine and Gabriella stares straight ahead at the wall but the only thing you can hear is Charlie's cornet weeping. And then Dorothy sets down the magazine and takes a deep breath and says, "Well, I've been imposing on you folks long enough, thank you for the hospitality." And she thanks me for the tea as well and walks out the door.

Gabriella is still sitting on the couch, drinking her coffee and chewing slowly on a pear, when I look down from the window and see Dorothy, in a camel coat and carrying two large suitcases, get into a taxi. I don't say anything. And then Peter and Felicinada stumble out into the street, tripping and laughing all over one another. I watch them until they disappear behind a row of parked cars. I can still hear them laughing. Gabriella bites into her pear and chews loudly. It seems to go on for hours.

## Gabriella (2)

What she said was: "You are com-pletely insane." This, as I was shaving, peering myopically into the mirror, grateful for the excuse to avert my eyes. She was sitting on the toilet with her legs crossed, looking at my reflection in the mirror. I couldn't meet even her reflected gaze.

I leaned closer and pulled against the side of my face to draw it taut over my jaw. I swiped at my chin with my razor, a Bic disposable. "Scrrch scrrch." It was a new razor and I liked how it pulled my whiskers evenly as it went. I pushed some shaving cream over to a spot I had just shaved and went over it again. Smooth as a baby's bottom. Up and around the lips, this can be tricky but you just have to take your time, be precise and be ready to back off if you think you're digging into skin.

"Are you listening to me?" she asked. The especially difficult part is the throat. I have this extra-prominent Adam's apple and so there's always this little outcrop of skin that just won't shave without being cut. My dad used a blade too. I guess the first razor I used, if you can count it, was his. My mother still describes how I emerged from the bathroom, five years old, tears welling up, shaving cream haphazardly spread across much of my upper thorax, blood everywhere, crying apologetically, "Something came happen to my lip." That's how she describes it anyway. He had one of those safety razors, with the knob on the handle that opened it up like a missile silo, to admit a new razor blade. "Safety razor"— I can only guess at what they could have meant, the things are a menace. Wilkinson Sword was my dad's brand. Generalizing from the cereal box experience, I was always under the impression that after you bought enough razor blades, you got one of those swords on the cover of the package. "Think of the pirate games that we could have with that thing," I thought, having learned nothing from my first bloodying.

"Yeah, I'm listening to you."

"Well, what the hell did you mean by what you just said?"

Despite my every precaution I felt the peninsula of skin carried off even as the shaving cream began to pinken. The effect was striking: crimson welling up through snow white. The ticket is to keep the skin as taut as possible; I cranked my chin around to the side as far as I could. I caught myself in the mirror, eyes way over to the side like a horse in fast water.

"Look, forget it," I said. Sccrrrch, sccrrrch, sccrrrch. "I'm still waking up here and," sccrrrch, "I was just mumbling away." I sneaked a peak at her. She was staring at the back of my neck without blinking, looking flummoxed. I looked away.

In the army there was this guy named Rainer in the same platoon as me in basic training. He was a Hutterite, or had been once. He used to use this straight razor that had been given to him by his grandfather. This thing had been sharpened so many times it was only about a half inch wide, although you could tell from the handle that it had originally been twice that. Rainer used to get up fifteen minutes before the rest of us to strop his razor against his belt. I still remember that singing sound it made as he slapped it back and forth and I'd know that in another half hour I'd be doing push-ups in the rain and I'd shudder. Rainer was bigger and stronger than any of us city kids and no one gave him any grief about anything even though he got drunk on two glasses of beer and couldn't speak to girls. And when he'd stand before the mirror with that razor, slow and contemplative, it looked to us like an unspeakably evil thing, and when he ran it down his face and no blood appeared, his stature grew tenfold. Within a month we had all gone out and bought one for ourselves to learn individually the compelling reasons behind the Gillette revolution. Some mornings we looked like we had fought all night with small delicate switchblades. When Rainer quit a week before the basic training was finished we were all astonished.

"Why do you think I spend so much time down here with you?" Sccrrrch, sccrrrch.

"I'll tell you why," she said. "It's because with you and me things are comfortable. There's no competition between us. We do not posture for one another and this is a very rare thing—lovers almost never have it, despite what they think sometimes. Let's please not mess this up."

Sccrrcch, sccrrcch.

Rainer quit, he said, because he figured out that this wasn't where he belonged. The rule was that if you finished basic training you had to finish out your four years but if you failed or quit basic training you could just walk away. Rainer said that it took him twenty-two years to walk away from the colony and only thirteen weeks to walk away from his promising career in the armed forces, so he figured that he was making progress.

After our final parade and after we had all got our postings, the platoon got together to drink together one last time. Someone asked if anyone knew where Rainer had gone. Someone asked why he had quit, did Sarge know? Sergeant Grabowski, eight years older than the rest of us, shook his head and said that Rainer was one of these guys who won't ever really belong anywhere, he knew the type, he said. The army is full of them.

"It's already messed up though, isn't it? I mean, from here on in I have to think about anything you say and anything I say . . . ah, shit." She stood up behind me. She looked like maybe she was going to start crying.

I remember watching him pack his little suitcase after he had turned in all his uniforms and everything. All he owned was a change of clothes and a Bible and his razor. He said he was going to look for construction work out west. I asked him if he knew anyone out there, he said he'd meet people. I gave him my parents' phone number in Dunsmuir but I knew I wouldn't see him again.

This was in 1989.

When his American wife had asked him to leave after the birth of their daughter, Leonard had been astonished and had had no reply available. To her, this looked like acquiescence to a reasonable request, but he could barely breathe over the pain in his belly, and for some reason, his jaw joints. He moved out in the space of a few hours, and the whole time he was afraid he was going to collapse.

This trivial boy his wife had taken up with disgusted him; her affection for the boy made Leonard question his own affection for his wife. Briefly. Optimistically. But she had long ago taken possession of him and there was no solution to this problem.

One year after the young Canadian had gone back to North America, he found himself in an airport lounge in Frankfurt, waiting for a connection. Giselle was there, with her father, and she recognized him. He was reading a novel, but became aware that he was being stared at. She looked different than she had and he did not recognize her. Leonard's face was behind a newspaper. Giselle waved. He waved back.

When she and her father returned to Paris, Giselle caught her mother alone and told her about seeing the boy, about his not recognizing her. Her mother breathed deeply and then stood straight and light for what seemed to her daughter to be the first time. Giselle wanted to say more, to enhance this effect, but she was older now, and knew enough to stop.

# SICK IN PUBLIC

## Part One

The year my twin brother, Albert, and I turned sixteen we each grew four and a half inches and nearly bankrupted our parents, our mother claims, so frequently were we thrusting our gaping maws into the refrigerator and chewing and swallowing. We both worked after school and weekends at the Red River Esso service station, and for our meal breaks we went across the street to the Dairy Queen. On any individual day we usually spent the bulk of our earnings there. It makes me queasy even now to think of it: triple burgers with chili and cheese, Peanut Buster Parfaits, Dilly Bars, onion rings, Super Dawgs, and on and on. We would phone ahead to avoid wasting eating time, pay wordlessly, sit down across a table from each other, and work our arms in synchrony, our mandibles a blur of insectoid frenzy. I'm sure we paid for the best part of the Dairy Queen's heating bill that winter. The girls behind the counter, who we knew from school, regarded us with the same pitying affection they might have had for a deformed baby pig. We didn't even notice them unless they got something wrong with the food. Like, broken glass in the ice cream might have got our attention.

The Dairy Queen was owned by a man named Terry, who was in his early forties and struck our father as something of an operator. Terry quickly got to know Albert and me, of course, and affected a friendliness that seemed genuine.

The thing about the Dunsmuir Dairy Queen was that it did far worse in summer than in winter—"the only one in the district!" Terry would wail, head in hands—the summer ice cream market having been wrapped up since the Eisenhower era by the Snak Shak and its Marshmallow Monsters. Terry had to do something about this and decided to sponsor a banana-split-eating contest.

His first idea was to have us compete as a team somehow, like the Genocidal Geminis on TV wrestling. Albert was mortified. "No, Terry. No, no, no, no. We won't even consider it," he said, leaning back from the table, gesturing with his tub of fried stuff.

Terry looked crestfallen.

"When exactly were you thinking of having this thing?" I asked.

Albert looked at me, appalled.

"Canada Day," Terry said, brightening.

"How would the rules work?"

Albert put his head down on the plastic table. At the counter Daphne Hainscotter wrinkled her nose. She'd have to wipe down that table, later.

And the next thing I knew Terry bet eight hundred dollars on me with Harold Simpson, the owner of Dunsmuir Florists. Terry and Harold had a rivalry going way back, something about Harold's ex-wife, since departed (for Montreal), and the Fun Mountain Water Slides. The details were obscure to me, only hinted at by my mother, who would then declare that we really shouldn't be talking about other people's business. The matter apparently had made for pretty interesting Chamber of Commerce meetings.

There was no way on earth that Terry was going to lose this bet and endure the consequent humiliation from Harold. My natural talents notwithstanding, he started me on a training regimen. After I closed up at the gas station, I would cross the street to the now darkened DQ. The back door would be left open for me and I would feel my way through the food prep area, around the grills and coolers, and emerge in the darkened Customer Service Zone. Terry would be waiting for me there, drinking rye whisky out of a milkshake cup, smoking cigars. Before him would sit half a dozen splits. And a stopwatch.

The secret, we established, was learning to avoid the maraschino cherries. You're already asking quite a bit of your poor gut—all that ice cream, the bananas, of course, the sauce, the sprinkly bits—and then you bite down on that maraschino cherry and that sticky red syrup hits the hangy-down thing at the back of your throat and, well, game over. So the technique we devised ended up with me going down on the ice cream mound and sliding the cherry off with the back of my spoon, taking up the scoop of ice cream in one bite and then knocking the next cherry down into the pool of melting ice cream. In the heat and fuss of the contest, we agreed, no one would notice. This technique emerged over long weeks of practice and stopwatching. It gave me new respect for the subtleties of things, the details you never notice.

Waiting for the morning bus that spring, Albert asked me over and over if I was really going to go through with it. Hell, how was I to know? "Yes, I really am going to go through with it," I said. After which a couple more cars would roar past us, down the highway. Luckier kids than us, taking their cars to school.

"You're being humiliated, you know."

"Am I."

"I just can't see why you're doing this."

"Because maybe you don't know everything, or even me, half as much as you think you do."

He stared at this wounding. I fished out a cigarette and shifted on my seat on the mailbox. The school bus pulled up. We both got on, and stared out the windows.

The week before the contest, Terry put me on a fast: saltine crackers and water. "You've got to be kidding," I said, eyes opening wide, smiling my best I'm-in-the-company-of-a-madman smile.

"Not even a french fry," he said to Daphne and the rest of the counter girls, who all looked on sympathetically. Who could be so unkind to a poor deformed baby pig? "And I'm just across the street. I'll know if a pizza car pulls up," he added, as I slumped out of the Dairy Queen and back to the gas station. Saltines. Jeez.

Which isn't to say that I subscribed completely to his rules, but in that week I still didn't take in anything like the quantity of food that my swelling body was used to—I felt weak and unsteady, I verged constantly on passing out. In history class I held a cloth to my face, across the room from Albert, who sat reading *Das Kapital*, completely oblivious to Miss Lindsay and her end-of-year ruminations on what really was the matter with young people today.

The weekend of the contest our parents decided to go visit relatives in northern Alberta. "Why do you suppose that would be?" Albert asked me, after this news had been relayed to us. I shrugged. There was really only one response: the neighbours spoke in scandalized terms, for years after, of the damage wrought upon their flower beds, the front lawn. They could only imagine what our house looked like inside, after. That was for sure.

I remember a few things. I remember talking to my friend Lester Phillipson in the garden about summer peas and how there likely wasn't anything better in the world, and him agreeing. I remember, I would be reminded of, the eleven—some accounts say thirteen— bottles of beer. I remember dancing in the front garden with some of Albert's friends, who were enacting *Le Sacre du Printemps*, me not understanding, but being indulged as one of the hosts anyway. I remember pressing twenty dollars into the hands of my sober friend Ross Paddock and insisting that he go down to the Kentucky Fried and get me—me who had been subsisting on half rations for a week—a barrel of Kentucky Fried Chicken, two whole chickens, a tray of those rolls that turn into paste on the roof of your mouth, a carton of the grey gravy, a mound of the sweet-as-molasses coleslaw. I remember all that.

Waking up on the front lawn. Sun. Hot. Thin film of perspiration stinging everywhere. Musty mouth. Throbbing red-hued world.

Mid-afternoon. Oh. My. God. The contest started. Ten minutes ago. The lawn lurching as I find my feet, my shoes, what are these *eggshells* doing here? Jesus God. Keys in truck. That was a mistake, starts. My God, fifteen minutes late already.

Pulling to a stop in front of the Dairy Queen. Big crowd all watching Floyd, the Dunsmuir Florists entry. Floyd, who was three hundred pounds easy and from way north of town but who had quit school in grade ten and so had almost been forgotten about, so rarely did we see him in town anymore, Floyd was starting to—rumble. The crowd grimaced and groaned and stood back a little. He had eaten seven banana splits. The eighth was in front of him, melting into a row of concentric circles of ice cream and syrup and sprinkly bits. And bananas and maraschino cherries.

Terry leaning into my face and barking, "You turkey!" Me blinking. Propelled through the crowd. Out of which appears a picnic table with a placard with my name on it. Melting banana splits lined up in rows. And then I'm sitting at the picnic table and everybody is still watching Floyd and nobody even realizes I'm a contestant, just Terry staring at me, looking betrayed, and then I start eating. I remember looking around as my head bent and my arm began scooping—push off the cherry, scoop, scoop, push off the cherry, scoop, scoop—and the crowd chatting and watching Floyd out of the corner of their eyes, warily, and I finished

77

one and started on another without even a breath. This was just muscle memory now. So many darkened nights inside, Terry smoking his cigar, me slurping—push off the cherry, slurp, slurp, push off the cherry, slurp, slurp—there wasn't even any consideration involved in it anymore, just my mouth opening and closing, swallowing. And then I was on my third and the crowd began turning to watch me and I was just a blur now, one windmilling arm and a stream of ice cream arching into my mouth and two halves of a banana besides. And by the fourth they were starting to clap with each spoonful—push off the cherry, scoop, clap, scoop, clap, push off the cherry—I'd never eaten like this in training and I was only accelerating. And by the fifth they were chanting *Bob, Bob*, with each scoop. And when I reached for the sixth the dads were holding their children above the heads of the crowd to see, and I saw out of the corner of my eye Daphne Hainscotter, standing in the front row, wearing her pink sundress, and oh my goodness, she was smiling wide right at me and my arm just whirled faster and my mouth sputtered and engulfed all the faster and I saw her and she was looking right at me. Daphne Hainscotter, shy and dignified, with *such* posture. Daphne, who in twelve years of attending school with me might have said ten words to me, news it was to me she even recognized my existence, and there she was, smiling right at me. Daphne.

And now the crowd was going crazy and Floyd knew he had to do something and kept picking up his spoon and sort of waving it but he wasn't going nowhere. And I whirled through the seventh and there it was, the eighth, all I had was one more, and Terry was bellowing, "Right on, Bob!" and all the DQ staff were there and now they were waving picket signs Terry had made them make up, saying EAT BOB, EAT and BITE THAT BANANA, and I held it up before the crowd triumphantly and set it down—the crowd loved that little bit of theatrics—and I picked up my spoon and looked right at Daphne, who yelled out, *"Go Bob!"* at the top of her shy and dignified lungs, and I looked right at her and smiled and she smiled too and I scooped a spoonful of ice cream. And bit down. On a maraschino cherry.

The arc of partially melted ice cream, bananas, sprinkly bits, and syrup shone like a rainbow, such was its multihued splendour. My head was a mortar tube, recoiling with successive discharges, and the first three rows of spectators were enveloped in a barrage of splits and Kentucky Fried Chicken and rolls that had turned to paste and grey gravy and coleslaw. And my paroxysm-racked body coiled and spun like a dropped fire hose and then I was on all fours and the river of rapidly liquefying ice cream was running down the sloped front lawn of the DQ and again and again and again, my eyes were shut. And finally someone put a wastebasket under me. And I nearly filled that too and finally there was nothing more. And it was dry heaving and it felt as though my body was turning inside out like a sport sock and then, nothing. I closed my eyes and groaned. A hand was on the small of my back, another on my shoulders. I reached into the garbage basket and picked out my glasses. I lifted my head and turned to her. Him.

"How are you doing?" Albert asked, smiling gently.

I nodded.

"Wanna go home?"

I nodded.

We stood and someone called my name and I looked around for her and the photographer from the *Dunsmuir Enterprise* leaned into me and flashed my photo, which ran on the front page that week under the headline "Miracle Comeback Pukes Out."

And Albert took me home and cleared some room among the beer bottles and put me to bed. I spent the rest of that weekend lying there, listening to him clean up.

## Part Two

The Dunsmuir and District Community Hall is used for dances, auctions, parades on rainy days, and particularly popular funerals. Albert and I had been in it probably a hundred times before our high school graduation dance.

The decorations committee, headed by Patti Nixon, six feet tall, three wide, and hair like Betty Crocker's

Creamy Vanilla Icing, did a fine job all that week beforehand, disappearing from the imponderably slow late-June-after-exam classes. In those languid days the decoration committee's excuses were not challenged, even when they returned in their boyfriends' cars drunk and voluble. The teachers competed with us students in distractibility, those last weeks: the college kids were already identified as such and they knew where they were heading and what really mattered. Which was to say: not this. And for the rest, the same. Nothing could have seemed to have less to do with the rest of our lives than those last weeks of empty silent hallways and lockers being cleaned out. There were half a dozen weddings planned for that summer; when the teachers shook their heads about these the maids of honour rankled indignantly. The brides said nothing at all, just sat there, frozen.

And my brother, who had learned that he hadn't after all won the chemistry prize or the history prize, but was headed off to a scholarship and an apartment of his own nevertheless, was suddenly possessed of an equanimity serene and confident, looking evenly at and smiling widely in the faces of the puffed-up gym teachers and princes and princesses of fashion in the cafeteria.

Every day in the shop that week Mr. Budwinski excused himself even earlier than was his habit and my friend Lester and I would make our way out to Lester's car in the student parking lot. Lester had decided to join the air force and had gotten his letter of offer a month previously; he knew for sure where he was headed. We sat out there in our smoky haze, considering our futures and the ripped interior of Lester's '64 Malibu four-door.

"The thing is." Cough. "Life is way. Longer. Than we think." Cough. "Here you go. We're so young we think that each moment is absolutely crucial. But life is long and you're allowed to change your mind. Thanks. If you don't. Like your first choice. You do something else."

"I guess."

"You're not getting uptight about all this graduation stuff, are you?"

"No, no."

"Because you shouldn't, you know."

"I'm not."

"Good."

"Uh-huh."

"How do you suppose they get these mirrors to stick to the windshield so well?"

"Krazy Glue?"

"Ever see one fall off?"

"Never."

"Got anything to eat in here?"

On the night of the graduation, Lester surprised us all by bringing Charlene Goffman. Brain-stallingly pretty, she had to be the surliest creature imaginable—at least within the hearty and false collegiality of our small-prairie-town frames of references. She had passed twelve years of public education in a nearly continual sulk. In the ninth grade she had made it nearly to January without smiling. She walked in that night with such disdain etched upon her features you'd have thought she had soiled herself. And when Lester came up to me before the dinner, eyebrows raised, rented tuxedo and scarlet bow tie still pressed and crisp, I held out my palms in mute astonishment. I hunched my shoulders to underscore my question.

"I know. But she said yes."

Even my brother was accompanied by crazy-as-a-coyote Cora, who dressed always in black, smoked Gitanes, lived in her own apartment in town, and had been only tenuously affiliated with the school for the last two years but who, in one of those spring-of-grade-twelve triumphs of pragmatism over principal, was graduated anyway. Cora had come over and met my delighted parents that afternoon, even asking my mother for the recipe for her strawberry trifle, my brother snorting into his hand, Mother looking at him, "Now don't you be rude, Albert," and later, in the kitchen to me: "Isn't it *wonderful?*" Cora, with her cat's-eye sunglasses and green lamé dress, pumps glittering, spoke more words that afternoon than I'd heard her utter in twelve years of shared stupor in the Lord Dunsmuir school system.

Before dinner was served and while the shrill gradu-
ates were all milling about, Lester sat with me on the
front steps of the community hall. Dinner was Chicken
Kiev, inevitably. His date, Charlene, was talking to her
friends around the big round table they had annexed.
Lester had thought that they would sit with me and
some of the rest of the power mechanic guys, but that
had been impossibly naive and he had settled for making the first excuse he could think of and joining me
outside. I was close to drunk already and sipping on the
mickey of rum in my pocket. Datelessness wasn't all that
bad, we agreed.

People were still arriving. Shiny older brothers' con-
vertibles with Kleenex flowers, a limousine—oh yeah,
son-of-the-dentist Dennis. Jerk. Falling out of the back,
loud and enormously entertained by himself. Yeah, yeah,
hi Dennis. Carol. Can you get by? Dennis played goalie
for the town junior A hockey team, the Fishermen. The
guys on the Fishermen all had had their jersey numbers
tattooed on their earlobes the weekend before. Jesus
God. And they all had dates, needless to say.

"I saw your brother inside," Lester said.

"Yeah."

"He's some drunk, him and his girlfriend."

"They were drinking together this afternoon already,
out behind the toolshed. They've just kept going."

"They're having fun, anyway."

"Great."

And then another car pulled up, driven by a friendly fat man I recognized to be Daphne Hainscotter's father. Daphne got out, leaned inside the car for maybe half a second, and shut the door. Lester and I split apart on the steps like a train was about to roar down between us. She glided into the hall without a glance or word to either side. Lester looked over at me, eyebrows raised, and handed me the mickey of rum.

Albert sat down between us. "Hi, Albert," Lester said. "Having fun?"

"Oh yeah," Albert said, breathing out a cloud of red wine vapour.

"Hi, Albert." Me, looking into the night, drinking from the mickey.

Albert: "This is gonna be some night." Lifting a bottle of red wine to his lips. Must have swiped it from our parents.

Lester, with detachment: "No doubt thirty years from now it'll seem to have been a pretty big deal."

"Won't take thirty years."

I turned to look at Albert. Something up. Lester talking about how his parents paint a picture of well-scrubbed optimism and hope but when he looks at their class pictures he knows half the people there, still in Dunsmuir, various versions of disappointed ambition and unacknowledged alcoholism, and Lester wonders why the night doesn't seem a little sadder to them.

"What won't take thirty years, Albert?"

"You really have no idea," he asked, stated. He started to rock back and forth. I looked at him. Then, with an effort, he climbed to his feet and stumbled back inside. Lester and I watched him go.

"We should maybe keep an eye on him," Lester said.

When Albert and I were four years old we both came down with strep throat. It seemed to have been clearing up, my mother says, when she noticed that I was looking sicker again, and then sicker yet, and then she saw I was peeing blood and she took me to the doctor and he said I had some inflammation of the kidneys, a complication of the strep throat, and that I would have to go into hospital. I did, my mother says, and I took it all well until I learned that Albert wouldn't be staying with me and then I just howled. It was the first time we were ever more than twenty feet from one another. My mother tells this story more and more often these days, now that we hardly see each other, and keep tabs on one another mostly through her. This tortures her, that we are no longer close, and she imagines that it is even more painful for her than it is for the two of us.

It was a big problem that I was so agitated, as my blood pressure was already dangerously high, from the kidney trouble. My mother stayed with me initially, and I tantrummed all night long that first night, and the next night my father stayed with me and I was even worse. It came almost as a relief to us all when Albert developed the same complication and peed blood too. We were put in the same room, and slept in the same bed, the night he was admitted. The rest of the month that we were in the hospital, we were angels together, my mother says. She always tears up at this point.

The meal took less than a coughing, dropped forked and napkinned hour. There were the speeches, by the class president, the chairperson of the grad committe, the principal, and all that. The speeches were chewy, the chicken impenetrable. For dessert, pineapple upside-down cake. I looked across the room to Albert and Cora, who were finding one another enormously entertaining, in that drunken way, the teachers at their table clucking their tongues, they couldn't even be quiet for the principal, much less the pineapple upside-down cake.

And Lester and Charlene looked like end-of-Lent gourmands, so desperately did they fill the time with chewing and swallowing and drinking their water and adjusting and rearranging the cutlery.

Daphne sat at a table with the other unaccompanied girls, carefully sawing at her Chicken Kiev in her serious and cautious way. I looked over at her often but each time her gaze was fixed upon her porcelain and if she looked up at all during the course of her meal, I didn't see it.

And after dessert, the dancing: Cora and Albert, careening around the dance floor. Lester and Charlene

dancing—Lester twitching with the grace and enthusiasm of a man in the electric chair, Charlene trying to
melt into the crowd around him, mortified, contem-
plating escape.

I drifted from corner to corner on the periphery of
the jerking mass, talking to classmates that I had liked
or admired, Daphne always seeming to be in the
opposite corner; all the auto mechanic guys talked to
me, and most of the teachers, too. And then someone
seizing my arm and flinging me into the twitching
tux-clad young men and their appalled companions;
my heart leaped at the prospect of some last-minute
confession of ardour and then bodies attached to the
seizing arm swing into view and Albert and Cora
grinning in my face. And I nodded and smiled and
began jerking in sympathy with the ruffle-neck-shirted
ones around me.

"Hi!" Cora yelled at me.

"Whoopee!" Albert yelled.

"Having fun?"

They nodded. "I'm gay!" Albert yelled at me.

"I said, having fun?"

"I mean I'm a fag!" Albert.

I smiled stupidly.

"What?"

"I'm a fag, I like to kiss men!"

"Oh," I said, nodding my head like a pendulum running down.

I looked over at Cora. She had her eyes shut, was gyrating to the strains of "Born in the USA." "Why are you telling me this now?"

But his answer was drowned out by some girl shrieking as she was held aloft, a grinning young man below her, she sitting on his shoulders, his head and torso obscured by yards and yards of taffeta.

And I danced the heck out of there.

I wound up over by the bar, leaning against the wall looking at but not watching the crowd, feeling faintly nauseous. We had dated the Smithson sisters in grade ten. For about a week, but still. "I like kissing men," he had said. I pictured it. In living colour. Which ones, I wondered.

Lester's favourite song that year was playing, a John Cougar Mellencamp number with fiddles and a deep-seated feeling for the land, and Lester was whirling and twirling and flailing like an overwound wind-up toy. He had hung his tux jacket on the back of his chair and sweat stains sagged from his armpits nearly to his belt. Charlene was dancing with several of the other girls, in the same room, anyway. And Albert and Cora, just on the other side of them, bumping and grinding.

Buying a bottle of Pepsi at the drinks table in front of me was Daphne, reserved and detached. She looked at me. I looked away for a flash. I looked back, she was still looking at me. I gave her a tight-lipped smile, she didn't smile back, I looked away. I looked back and she was standing right in front of me. "Hi, Bob," she said.

"How are you, Daphne."

"Fine, thank you. What are you doing in the fall?"

"Finding work here, I hope, doing a heavy equipment mechanic's apprenticeship."

"And your brother?"

"He's going to university. Chemistry. You?"

"I'm going to Montreal to study English."

"Great. Seems like I'm the only one here who'll still be here next winter."

"Seems that way."

"So you're quitting the DQ."

"Last week."

"Think you'll miss it? Were you close to the other people there?"

"We pretended to be but weren't really. I don't think we'll keep in touch."

I nodded. This much proximate observation was starting to overwhelm me. Daphne had for so long been the feminine ideal, her splayed feet, square bony shoulders, body by Lego, all right angles and perfectly erect neck, I was starting to choke and spit in the ambrosial waters, drowning in the idyll.

There was something up on the dance floor, probably some drunken hockey players starting to fight. Nothing to do with me. "Um," I said, glancing between her and the fuss. She waited for me to say whatever it was I was having so much trouble with. "Um . . ." Lester touched my elbow.

"You'd better do something about your brother before he gets himself killed," he said.

"What?" I said, irritated, with a can't-you-see-who-I'm-talking-to-here look. He pointed.

" 'Scuse me," I said, again and again, wending my way between the compacted and slippery dancers. " 'Scuse me, 'scuse me." And then I was beside Cora, who was laughing drunkenly, shrilly, at Albert, who was walking with exaggerated finger-to-shushed-lips steps among the crowd. And Mitchell Garson, a left-winger destined for the Quebec Nordiques, was stamping through the crowd, bull-necked and snorting, and I looked back at Albert just in time to see him lean over and plant a kiss on the lips of son-of-the-dentist Dennis, who looked around initially with a self-congratulatory smile and then eyes open wide and wiping his face and lunging after Albert, who ran behind a knot of bare-stockinged girls dancing in a circle, Albert yelling, "Woo-hoo, woo-hoo, woo-hoo," Cora squealing with delight, Albert running over to us—and right into Mitchell Garson's cantaloupe-sized fist, Albert falling. I closed my eyes for a long second.

The strobe light was flashing away now to "Ballroom Blitz," Mitchell Garson was shading his eyes with a hand and still snorting and searching in syncopated, staccato movements. Albert appeared beside me, staggering and holding his nose, blood running down the side of his face in an interrupted, mechanical progression. Albert not saying anything.

"Let's go," I said.

"Whatsamatter," he protested, holding his nose, as I guided him to the door.

"Time to lie down, Albert," I said.

"Whyyy?"

"Because." Sympathetic onlookers, who had perhaps not seen his dance-floor antics, smiled at me. Every year there's always a few.

Daphne was standing beside the door as I guided him out.

"Anything the matter?" she asked.

"Just doing some baby-sitting," I said. She nodded, disapproving.

We made our way out into the night. It was just after solstice and, even at midnight, there were still a few orange clouds in the west. Albert stumbled and staggered and it was all I could do to guide him over to the hedgerow that bordered Saunders's pasture. Some instinct for self-preservation must have endured the soaking with wine, because he stumbled without much protest to the elm I selected and laid his head down on a root.

And within a minute he was snoring and sputtering and as motionless as Dunsmuir on a Sunday afternoon.

Climbing the steps back into the community hall, the last few dances crooning down that stairway to heaven, I am seized by the shoulders and slammed nostril-first into the side of the stairway, I smell ammonia and I am spun around and just manage to get my arms in front of my face and they're squished up against my nose and eyes and all I can see and taste and smell is the insides of my elbows, slammed into my face by five or six swings of what feels like a large shovel. "I'm not *him*," I yell through my arms but it comes out stuttering and weak like the sound a won't-start lawn mower makes. And then one arm and then the other is peeled off me and he winds back. "Fuck you!" I yell at him. "Open your eyes!" And he stops.

"It's not him, Mitch," somebody says. Mitch snorts and spins on his heel and jumps down the steps and I lose sight of him in the night. I listen for Albert but all I hear is Mitch breathing hard. His coterie of the outraged troops down the steps to resume their pursuit. Mary Lou Waters leaning into my face—"He mighta given Dennis *AIDS!*"—drawing out that last like it had four syllables, Dennis turning white, Mary Lou comforting him. I slip around them and into the hall. Cora sitting in the corner drinking from a bottle of amber Pepsi and talking to herself. Daphne not in sight, gone home I guess, story of my life. Lester and Charlene rubbing their uvulas on the dance floor.

Cora smiling as I sit down beside her. She hands me her Pepsi bottle. No words between us. Lester sits down beside us, wiping his mouth.

"Howd-y pard-ner," Cora says, giggling madly to herself.

Lester's hand pauses above the bottle, asking permission. I nod. "Is your brother okay?" he asks as he takes a long swallow.

Cora puts her head down on the table and giggles. "Right as rain," she says. Lester looks at me. Half-smile.

"He's just taking a nap now."

Lester nods.

"Poor thing's probably just overtired," Cora says to the table. Lester rolling his eyes. Me leaning back in the chair.

And then Daphne: "Mind if I sit down? How's your brother doing?"

"Cheerful as a chicken," Cora says from the table, laughing.

Me: "He's just fine."

Daphne furrowing her brows at Cora for an instant, then turning to me. Lester looking around to see where Charlene got to. Oh well.

Daphne: "Is someone taking care of him?"

Me: "He'll be okay, he's sleeping it off. In the morning he probably won't remember any of this."

Cora's laughing made a bubbling sound, in the spilled drinks on the table. Lester looked at her and then at us and laughed a little too. Daphne just looked at me. And I looked at Albert, staring in at us from the

night-shiny window, motionless, hands on glass, neither smiling nor frowning, just looking. From across
the lawn behind him, you could see Mitchell Garson
running.

This was in 1984.

When Robert moved to Montreal from the prairie he had never lived alone before. He spent three days looking for an apartment and when he found one he liked he rented it and had the keys in his pocket within an hour. It had wooden floors that gleamed in the afternoon sun.

There were people he knew from home who had moved there but he didn't seek them out, choosing to refashion himself in a way that would not be credible to someone who had known him as a child, especially his brother. He bought and tried to read difficult books, and studied the book reviews to learn what he should be concluding from them. He learned French and he learned which accent he should affect. He adopted mannerisms that would have been deemed absurd on the prairie. They were absurd here, too, but the city was more tolerant of fops.

He became preoccupied with appearing interesting to people. He claimed to have been in the Foreign Legion, and to have walked across the Darien Gap. He said that he spoke Swahili. He decided to study the hermeneutics of literary theory. He didn't even know what that phrase meant. He was twenty-three, just.

When his father came to visit, he and his newly foppish son had even less to say to one another than they once had, when the boy would hang around his father's garage workshop. The boy was ashamed to have his father see his new clothes and hear his half-baked ideas, and he turned that shame into embarrassment over his father, though no one in the city would have found the older man any more improbable than his son.

They ate lunch together and the father asked him what he was studying and how his classes were going. The boy spoke at length about German ideas about text and identity and class. He kept using the fact that these ideas were German to account for the imprecision with which he described them. The father left mystified. It was the boy's last chance, really, to save himself, and he ignored it.

# INSOMNIA, INFIDELITY, AND THE LEOPARD SEAL

Mornings for the emperor penguin are even worse. In the Antarctic dawn they stir, stretch their wings, squawk sleepily to those around them, and head down to the edge of the ice floe, to do something about breakfast. Something in the way of *Eugenia superba*, which teem in the waters of the southern oceans and constitute the emperor penguin's principal food source. Trouble is, as the mob of still-waking penguins approaches the water's edge they start to remember about the leopard seal. For the leopard seal, breakfast is emperor penguins. So the penguins all stop right at the water's edge and lean way over and look real hard for the leopard seals, who of course are not nearly so stupid that they'd give any suggestion of their presence. The classic Homeric quandary: to breakfast and test one's mortality or to fast and fear.

The penguin equivalent of bacon and eggs, without the fruit salad cop-out option.

These quandaries can only go on so long, of course, and soon the penguin mob starts to get a little restless. What to do? What happens is: the ones at the back start pushing.

There is a great shriek of indignant protest, much scrambling and flailing about, and eventually—a splash. Everything stops. The penguins lean over, way over, watching silently. The penguin in the water stares around, at first with a terrified and then with sort of a self-righteous see-it's-not-so-bad type of look, and then there's a stirring in the water and a cloud of red. The other penguins all back up quickly.

And after the Real Life Nature Drama, there was the Prayer Hour and a Half and then the Home Shopping Channel—a dozen ice cube trays for twenty dollars, who'd have imagined such bargains could still be had? Heading into the third hour of late-night television, who knows what beauty is? Even fifteen minutes of sleep would be paradise. In lieu of that, live rugby from Australia. The Newbridge 'Nihlators versus the Bainsbury Brick Bats. Bring it on.

They speak of sleep hygiene. Just as eating from each of the four food groups, brushing after every meal, and tending to your cuticles are habits that will pay dividends the whole of your adult life, so too will your nighttime equanimity be maintained by observing the following rules: No napping. Retire and arise at roughly the same time each day—no weekend slumberfests. No eating and no reading in bed. If you can't sleep, after one hour get up and do something until you feel tired. No heavy physical exercise after 6 p.m. No eating within two hours of retiring. Minimize nicotine and caffeine use. Resist alcohol or sedatives for short-term relief—you just end up with a hangover the next morning, might as well have not slept. Try running or long walks earlier in the day. And if all this fails, ask yourself, is there something else bothering you? Is everything okay at work? Is there any particular reason why you haven't set foot outside your apartment in a month, except to go to work and pay the pizza delivery guy?

Disturbances of sleep and mood have cause and effect wrapped around one another like two snakes on a stick. Very often trouble manifests itself initially and insidiously, through very-early-morning awakening, and only later does the visible darkness close in around one's bed. What more telling a development for someone teetering on the brink of something than to spend a week wide awake at four in the morning, recollecting and recriminating? Streetlight shining in through night-lit window, empty ache in abdomen, throat feeling swollen and full.

My wife's disposition is so retina-searingly bright, most people think her intoxicated or deranged on first meeting. She has no patience for melancholy friends of ours.

"You have to take responsibility for how you feel," she'd say. "Feelings don't just happen to you, they are chosen things, and they're part of how you make yourself. If people choose despair, they're not just sad, they're wrong. And need to be told so." On the matter of a neighbour of ours who left his wife and infant daughter for a bartender he claimed to have never wanted to fall in love with: "Bullshit, Robert. If he stopped meeting her and fucking her on her futon, he'd fall out of love with her quickly enough. It's just will." You'd think that, knowing all this, I'd have had some insight when she herself began rising to drink tea at the kitchen table in the very early morning.

The coordination and supervision of sleep is handled by a structure in the brain stem, called the reticular activating system, that is remarkable in that it exists in no one anatomic spot but rather throughout the brain stem, everywhere at once, like a shudder perhaps, or a sponge in gelatin. What it does when it is time to sleep is shut down the transmission of sensory input beyond the brain stem, allowing the cerebral cortex to turn inward and reel and dance and analyze the day's experience in sweet reverie. It retains the option, however, to transmit sudden fluctuations in input—such as an alarm clock, or a spouse slipping into bed hours after she said she'd be home—up to the cortex for analysis. From an evolutionary point of view its development probably served two purposes: going to sleep for the night kept us curled up in the fork of a tree silent and inconspicuous and conserving energy, not drawing the attention of predators better adapted than we are to manoeuvring in the night. And as mammals grew cleverer and cleverer, the need for the brain to be able to sit back and integrate subtle lessons and clues became greater. We infer this second purpose of sleep and dreaming from the fact that infants spend most of their day sleeping and most of their sleep dreaming, while septuagenarians sleep half as much and their dreams flicker past them in a too familiar whisper. As the world grows more known, less musing and inferring is necessary.

The ability of the reticular activating system to induce sleep depends upon its capacity to act at inhibitory synapses along critical neural paths in the brain. When the reticular activating system discharges these inhibitory synapses, conduction slows and sensory input to the cerebral cortex is reduced. Synapses are connections between nerve cells. One nerve cell relays information to another by releasing a chemical signal near the other's receptor. This causes charged atoms—ions—to rush in or out of the cell, creating an electrical discharge. The secretion of an adequate amount of the chemical signal or neurotransmitter is critical to the entire process. The conceptualization of the blues that is presently most popular holds that it consists of a failure of certain nerve cells to secrete sufficient quantities of neurotransmitter. The strength and speed of signals through the brain are reduced and all the drives suffer: libido, hunger, and anger all fade to memory, leaving empty abdomen and imprecisely described despair.

The nearly universal presence of sleep disturbances among people with mood disorders suggests strongly that the signals of the reticular activating system are weakened as well by the dearth of neurotransmitter. Interestingly, it has long been noted that many mood disorders can be quickly ameliorated by enforced sleep deprivation—a tool of limited clinical use, as eventually patients wind up sleeping in a broom closet someplace and waking up bluer than blue can be.

The sleep disturbances produced by the blues are various and may include hypersomnia; a roommate I had in university once spent the month after flubbing his GMAT sleeping eighteen hours a day. He'd go for days on end without getting out of his housecoat. After a while it seemed I hardly had a roommate at all, so rarely did I see him vertical. More typically, however, insomnia is the problem; sometimes initial insomnia—difficulty falling asleep—but this is more usually related to poor sleep hygiene and stress/anxiety disorders. Classically, what is found is terminal insomnia: waking up in the very early morning unable to fall back asleep, despite one mind-numbingly inane infomercial after another until the sky in the east is lightening to the colour of a deep and recent bruise. And now, Martha,

I've got something really special for our shoppers. I don't think we've presented steak knives of this quality ever before. Handmade by traditional craftsmen in Thailand, you gotta know these are going to go fast. We have only three hundred sets of these beauties, so act now. Oh look, we have a testimonial on the line, so don't take our word for it, Richard from Hamilton how do you find these knives?

Nothing goes on forever. The emperor penguin can wait tortured on the ice floe for only so long and then he has to eat. And the traffic appears in the street and it's time to get dressed and go to work. And that whole day you'll answer questions with confused non sequiturs and everyone from the lady at the muffin stand to the paper boy will comment on how unwell you look.

Think about the leopard seal: hiding under the water beside the ice floe, wondering if this is the spot the penguins will choose that morning. Invisible only for so long as she can hold her breath, eventually she has to return to the surface too. Think about the look the penguins and the leopard seal exchange when she pops to the surface, gasping for air.

This was in 2004.

Robert and Paul learned later that they had been regulars at the Café Kiev at the same time. They were both students then, but they went to different universities: Paul to the Université de Montréal and Robert to McGill. In those days too, feelings ran high over the language debate and the separation referendum. Robert was wary of approaching strangers in that city, with his French so rudimentary and inflected with the prairies. He regretted his caution, in retrospect. When he met Paul later, through Daphne, he thought that he could have used a friend like him that first winter in Montreal.

Felicinada returned to the city two years later. Gabriella had gone back to Buenos Aires. Felicinada asked mutual acquaintances if anyone had forwarding addresses, but Gabriella had left behind no trace of herself. When Robert moved back to the city from Paris, with an improbable anecdote about a Parisian plumbing magnate and his ex-wife, he returned first of all to the café. He sat at a little table with his suitcase beside his feet and Felicinada walked up to him and they were cautious with each other, wondering if they were recognized. They each concluded they weren't, and he gave his order and she took it, not making eye contact, and when his food came all he did was nod.

It was only as he was leaving that he betrayed himself. "How long have you been back?" he asked. She told him. "Nothing is the same, is it?" he said. She said she thought that what had changed had done so obviously, and what remained was more subtle and more important.

Hearing her say that made him suddenly miss the little girl Giselle, and he told Felicinada what had happened in Paris. Everyone in the café eavesdropped. There was the smallest bit of sympathy for him.

# STRUCTURE IS CONSTANT

Cora turned her car into the curling rink parking lot and pulled up next to a snowbank. She let the engine idle for a while as she listened to the news. Only five in the afternoon and it was already dark. She shut off her headlights. The night sky lit up slowly like a just-plugged-in Christmas tree. She let the engine idle some more.

A truck pulled into the parking lot and out jumped a down-enveloped baby-blue Michelin Tire man who scurried into the rink with a rigid-armed waddle that spoke eloquently and precisely of the outside temperature. Cora shivered and turned up the radio. The prime lending rate was down a percentage point. Fighting in the Balkans; the Italian government looked as if it would fall. Cora heard another car door slam and then another parka-clad, sexless figure streaked past her, leaving behind a stream of breath vapour that lingered like an uncoiling leash. The snow glowed silver-blue under the night sky.

For the first time in her life Cora listened through all the football scores. "And it's only December," she said aloud. She had been living in the old suicide's house, and living his life, for six months already. She shut off the radio and then, reluctantly, the car heater.

Slamming the front door behind her, she paused to catch her breath in the curling rink cloakroom. The heavy laundry-hamper air of the rink rushed past her, and the sticky smell of whisky and cigarette smoke and candy was more welcome than it could have been on any warmer night. Pierre Lavallee was hanging his coat up.

"Hi, Cora," he said. "How's it going?"

"Just fine, thanks, Mr. Lavallee," she declared, noticing how sincere she sounded. "And how are you doing?"

"Oh, about the same, I suppose." He shrugged. "Like you said, it's gonna take time I suppose." There was a pause. He looked at Cora expectantly. She smiled stupidly. She blinked. She had no idea what he was talking about. Pierre shrugged again and hung his toque on a hook and walked into the bar. Cora stood with her hand still on her coat. Ringworm? Migraines? Depression? Impotence. Ever since his hog barn had . . . no that was Mr. Aizenman. Back pain? Jesus.

In the bar she surprised herself and ordered a rye and ginger. Incontinence? The rest of her rink wasn't there yet. She took a deep swallow and sat down to put on her curling shoes. (One with a rubber grip, the other with a slick plastic slider; the day she'd bought them she'd worn them home to break them in and zoomed over the sidewalk ice paddling away like a skateboarder late for school.) Cora had been in Pigeon River for about two weeks when it had become apparent to her that she had to do something to reduce the amount of empty time spent alone in the house. In the summer she had played softball with a huge ball and this rule that you couldn't strike out, you swung until you hit it. Which had made for some pretty long at bats but they had indulged her. And now she was learning to curl. *"CURLING!"* a friend from Montreal had squealed into the phone. "You mean, like, with kilts?"

"Yeah, yeah," she had replied. "Listen, it doesn't look like the Bolshoi is going to make it out here this winter and it gets claustrophobic here in the summer, never mind what January is going to be like." And so she had signed up for the clinic rink. (Teams are called rinks. Innings are ends. Four players to a rink, eight ends to a game. Never mind about keen and wick. No, you need a special curling broom, you can get them down at McCleod's Hardware.) The skip was Mrs. Dubinsky, the clinic nurse, the lead was her husband, Walt, who taught grade seven and lived for good jokes, and the second was Ed Harrison, the pharmacist, who, at thirty-three, still lived with his parents, who owned the drugstore but had promised to give it to him as a wedding present. Or so Mrs. Dubinsky had said. Ed seemed to say nothing at all.

It had been a month since the four of them had gone down together for the practice night. "Just go throw a few," Mrs. Dubinsky had said, "to get the weight of them, while we figure out who's gonna skip. We'll be right down. Walt, get over here." And so Cora had gone down to the ice while the others were debating and manoeuvring, not that it really mattered to them. "Just go throw a few, to get the weight," she'd been told. And so she did.

The first thing she got was that those things were way heavier than they looked. She held the curling stone against her abdomen and tried to figure out how anyone could actually throw the thing. She heaved it forward. The next thing she got was lumbar disc prolapse. The third thing she got was a growing realization that she had caught the attention of just about the entire curling club, partly from the two-foot gouge in the ice where the rock had landed and partly from the silent stares of everyone in the building, whose awed faces she could just make out from her prone position on the ice when she turned her eyes all the way to the side. If it weren't for the searing pain in her back, she might have been more embarrassed.

Later, as they were wheeling her out, she asked, "Well, why don't they just *say* 'push'?"

It looked like the gouge had been repaired, she noted out of the corner of her eye, not wanting to acknowledge it. Carl something, the rink attendant, waved to her and pointed to the spot, smiling, indicating with his hand that it had all been smoothed over. Cora smiled back at him over her Styrofoam cup and flapped her fingers at him. She turned around. He pointed that out every time she curled, just in case the episode still bothered her.

Her shoes now on, with a ludicrous pink furry bed-room slipper—courtesy of Mrs. Dubinsky—slipped over the left to protect the shiny smooth sliding surface, Cora walked to her locker and got her broom. She walked back to the lounge and had just picked up an issue of *Icesports Today* when Mrs. Dubinsky and Walt came in, followed by Ed Harrison.

"Cora!" Mrs. Dubinsky effused. "You're here early!" Cora put down the magazine thankfully.

"Well, we're all here," Walt observed. "Why don't we go"—eyebrows raised almost to his receded hairline—*"throw"*—mouth open now, eyes darting from side to side—"a few stones?"

"Now Walt, leave the poor girl alone." Mrs. Dubinsky slid an over-the-horn-rimmed-glasses look at him and they all hoisted their brooms and headed down to the ice to push some rocks around.

In a letter to the boyfriend who had refused to accompany her to Pigeon River, Cora had likened the town to one of those tanks they had read of in psychiatry experiments. "It's a fifteen-hundred-person sensory deprivation chamber, Mark. Please send me some old copies of the *Mirror*. Can I come visit soon?" But his reply had been vague and slow in coming and so she knew that things had changed and soon she stopped writing. "Error after error after error," she'd said aloud one morning at three, her head flat on her kitchen table, her eyes shut and streaked, a half-empty bottle of piña colada mix in front of her. "Mood Indigo" played for the thousandth time that night and Sarah Vaughan's feeling had gone right down her knees and she'd just sat and cried, "Go long, blues."

On the ice Cora listened as her teammates spoke earnestly of strategy, raising their eyes to her for her concurrence. She nodded thoughtfully. "Sure," she said. Cora understood curling as shuffleboard but on ice and with way heavier pucks. She liked it when a rock of the other team was in the bull's-eye, she meant house, because then all she had to do was hit their rock and everyone on her team, she meant rink, was satisfied, not to say surprised. Figuring out how hard to throw it to get it to stop on its own in the bull's-eye, she meant house, was an entirely different matter, however. And of course there is a very good reason that the game is called curling. At least in shuffleboard, when you throw the puck straight, it goes straight.

But this was easily the most social sport she had ever seen, she'd have to give it that. You could scoot around on the ice with a drink in your hand and no one thought anything of it. A cocktail party you could call a sport—great idea.

Afterwards they sat in the lounge savouring their first win of the year. Even Ed seemed happy. Walt was downright ebullient. It was all that Mrs. Dubinsky could do to stop him from getting up on the table and doing the cha-cha.

Driving home she noticed how the sky had clouded over the stars and how the wind had picked up. The ground drift formed a carpet of blowing snow maybe a couple of feet deep that swept over the highway continuously. Cora had to gauge where the road was by her position relative to the telephone poles on either side. She slowed down and leaned forward into the dash. She gripped the wheel tightly and felt for the edge of the pavement with her tires. She turned off the radio and breathed slowly.

When she pulled into the driveway she felt the snow squeak the way it does when it is fresh and especially cold. She drove slowly, listening to the chirping under her tires, and gently came to a stop in her garage. She shut off the engine and the lights. It was utterly black. She plugged in the car by feel and groped her way to the door. Once outside she sprinted to the front door of her house. Inside, she stood for a minute, shivering and shaking and waiting to warm up. She walked into the living room with her coat still on, the lights still off. Outside, along the highway, she saw a car pass by: first a diffuse lightening in the trees, then a rapidly narrowing cone of headlights, and then the car itself but only for an instant of metallic colour and red taillights and then it was gone.

The wind picked up further and little swirls of snow swept along inches off the ground outside. The sky seemed still lower, and in the direction of town, Cora could see it glowing yellow from the lights. A semi-trailer passed by outside, running lights blazing, charging into the night. Cora blinked as the room shone with its headlights. When it was black again she switched on the light. In the window she saw herself and the room reflected in the glass, and underneath all this she saw steadily moving beads of light that crept horizontally across the window. All that was missing was the rhythmic beeping.

She found the copper Canada-goose teakettle under the counter and set it on the stove, burnished wings outstretched as if to take off, or land, in her neat little kitchen.

The previous occupant of the house, David Andrews, had lived here for forty-eight years, the last thirty of them alone. He'd been seventy-six when he had died, a month before Cora had finished her family practice residency, forty grand in debt, exhausted, constantly frustrated with Mark. Andrews's kids had taken a few pictures and the silverware, and thrown the rest of the furnishings in with the house and the practice. They'd even left his shotguns neatly racked in the basement.

For Cora it had been like simply switching gears. One minute she was a harried resident in Montreal putting up with her unreliable boyfriend mostly because it's his name on the lease and the next, the clutch goes in and clunk, she's alone under the prairie sky of Manitoba, nothing taller than a grain elevator for four hundred miles in any direction, desperate for a cappuccino, stepping into the beloved Dr. Andrews's life. She was still finding notes he'd left for himself: "Don't forget the eggs," "Write Bonny," or, more mysteriously, "Mail the sparrows to liverwurst."

When Cora had been growing up in Dunsmuir, Manitoba, two hundred miles east of here, she had constructed her entire identity around the distinction between her and everyone else around her. She was born and raised in a place not very much different from this place, but by seventeen, she couldn't have been less familiar with curling, or down clothing, or the concept of self-sufficiency as an ideal if she had spent her entire life in the greater Montreal area. She dressed like a silage bale, wrapped in black vinyl, and for her date at the high school graduation dance she took the one gay boy in the school. Or the one who didn't keep it a secret, anyway. Her secret was also out by that time: she was not like anyone else there.

Her abrupt return to Manitoba following her residency surprised her as much as anyone. It was partly her boyfriend, but there were a hundred escape routes open to her from that particular problem. She tried to explain it to her friend Daphne, also from Dunsmuir, who was in the same residency program in Montreal: "It's like I'm not finished that course, or something. I'm still a few credits short, is how I feel."

"Listen, it was a shitty place. You have unresolved issues, let it go."

"I just think that if I did let it go, it's like, I'd never finish that degree, and all my life, I'd be wondering what was really in the course calendar."

"I can't say that I understand."

"Well, the money is good, they're paying for the move, and I think I just want to be an adult for a while."

"You have an unfulfilled yearning for parental approval."

"If you say so."

The copper Canada-goose teakettle began shaking with impatience. Spurts of steam started spraying out of its little nostrils and a high-pitched shriek began to sound from somewhere within it. She picked it up and directed its head at her cup of cocoa. The lower bill flopped open and out spurted a stream of boiling water. Cora stirred. Mrs. Andrews and the children had gone back east one Christmas in the early sixties and hadn't been on the train back. On her cup, "David" was spelled in Teutonic letters. She sipped her cocoa. Underneath that it said, "World's Greatest Golfer." A Christmas-party gift, maybe. This house must have seemed terribly quiet and empty for a long time. She looked at her about-to-take-flight kettle and shook her head. The cocoa was good.

She picked up a copy of the *New England Journal of Medicine* that sat on the kitchen table. A couple of formal studies of a new chemotherapeutic regime for ovarian cancer, a case report about a new type of fungus found to infect AIDS patients, and a review article on the management of post-myocardial-infarction heart failure. According to Dubinsky, Dr. Andrews had kept in touch with the kids, spoke of them often, and had brought them out for a few days each summer. Their various graduations had been high points for him. She stood and walked back into the living room, flipping through the heart failure article. He never explicitly spoke of his wife again, but Mrs. Dubinsky maintained that he never stopped missing her. The sequence that followed was familiar enough: never took another vacation, was always available for house calls, reassurance of new parents. And Mrs. Dubinsky never said anything that accounted for the boxes and boxes of empty Seagram's Five Star bottles in the basement. Cora shifted around on the overstuffed purple-and-yellow couch; it was the sort of furniture that would not allow you to be comfortable, no matter how much you squirmed.

The house was an archaeological dig—relics of different eras lying side by side but nevertheless distinct and datable to the practised eye. The couch, for instance,

Cora assumed to be of Mrs. Andrews's era—she must have been starved for colour. The purple-and-yellow couch, the Gauguin prints in the hallway—anything that was old enough to have been bought when she was around dripped colour like a box of sun-melted and faded Crayolas. And among these things, but entirely apart from them, were the subdued cowboy prints in the den, the dark wooden bookcases beside the fireplace—like ashes not quite covering spilled paint.

ACE inhibitors, diuretics, beta blockers, low-salt diets: there seemed nothing much new in the field of heart failure management.

Cora put down the journal and stretched. She was restless and having trouble concentrating. She was lonely. She decided not to call Mark. She walked to the fireplace and leaned her head against the mantel and shut her eyes.

In the bookcases beside the fireplace sat all of his old textbooks. From the publishing dates in them, Cora had established that he had gone to medical school from 1935 to 1940. Johns Hopkins, no less. The books were beautiful leather-bound hardcovers, with monochrome engravings protected by tissue paper, all carefully inscribed "Property of David A. Andrews." His handwriting had been neat and elegant, with none of the tremor apparent in his chart entries of the last couple of years.

When he'd gone to medical school, penicillin had not yet been available. TB had been consumption and essentially incurable. The most common cause of madness had been syphilis, and, with patience, one could talk schizophrenics out of their delusions. Every time Cora flipped through these books she learned something new. In 1939, they had thought they were right around the corner from curing lung cancer. And GPs did so much of their own surgery in those days—appendectomies, hernias, Caesarean sections; his surgery texts were magnificent, with beautiful colour plates and engravings with detail so fine you could have framed them. She could have prepared for her own exams from his anatomy texts. She recalled her gross anatomy prof introducing the course: "Structure, class, is the only constant. Learn it well once."

She wandered back into the kitchen. The decorations in here were mostly the kind you'd throw in the cart at Safeway to fill up the wall space, make it seem homier. A porcelain swordfish. Picture of some state capitol. He would have hoped for a bigger difference.

Down the stairs, turning on lights as she went. She found the door to the den and carefully felt for the desk lamp. The room smelled of pipe tobacco. On the wall just above the desk were several rectangles of lightened wallpaper—his old diplomas. Cora sat down in the big leather chair behind the desk. Above her there were six missing ceiling tiles—no amount of scrubbing could make them come clean. Through the hole she could see exposed wiring and the wooden floor joist, still frayed and stained dark brown. She leaned back in the chair, putting her feet up on the desk. It had been while looking at these walls that he had found his resolve. She crossed her arms in front of herself. Why then and not twenty years earlier? The phone rang. Long distance.

The first weekend she had stayed at his place: late summer and still so hot it felt like you couldn't get a full lungful of air. His place was on a leafy street in the McGill Ghetto, and his neighbours above and below him were friends of his. All Saturday afternoon they dropped by with invitations to eat and requests to borrow. She was too hot to contemplate walking anywhere, and so they stayed there and drank iced tea and lolled around on the floor. Between visits, she pushed him on his back, and he stretched his arms over his head and she just stared at what she had wrought, pulling up on the small of his back and burying her mouth in his belly. The girls upstairs came by without knocking and extracted a bottle of vinegar from the kitchen with hardly a glance at the enmeshed bodies on the living-room floor. The sunlight blazed all through the apartment.

The next day they watched a hardcore band at the Spectrum and sucked in the air-conditioned and smoke-laden air like they were sea mammals up from a very long and deep dive. The music shook the walls and somehow everyone in the room seemed to know one of them; nods greeted them from every quarter but it was too loud to explain who was who, even through a hollered-in ear. They ordered western sandwiches on white bread and drank Labatt Blue.

At the time neither of them understood how lucky they were.


Charging out into the snow, the wind still higher now, she couldn't even see the highway. The erosive cold clawed at her face, tears freezing against her cheeks, and the back of her throat hurt from breathing in the cold air so fast. Snow filled up her slippers and began melting against her feet, the wind swept up her shirt and her breasts hurt from the cold. She'd told him not to bother shipping the boxes to her, to just give the clothes to the Salvation Army. He'd asked why she was so upset. Had she thought he was going to keep her stuff indefinitely?

In front of her was a branch that had been broken off by the wind . . . elm, the size of an axe handle. She swung it against a snowdrift; it hardly slowed. Snow flew everywhere, and she spun around from her own momentum. She strode to the oak that dominated the driveway. She was standing in snow up to her mid-thighs now, shaking from the cold, her feet completely numb. She swung the branch into the tree. Frozen, it rang like metal and her hands hurt up to her elbows. She swung it again. It cracked and rang out. She swung it again. It gave way at the fracture and bent noiselessly, tendrils of bark and wood still holding the broken branch together.

She threw it into the snow. The air was so cold it smelled like ammonia.

This was in 2001.

It wasn't so bad, the divorce, or anyway it wasn't nearly as bad as it had seemed it would be. Robert left Montreal and made his way back to Manitoba that summer, without his wife, and mostly, no one even asked him about her. His friends were collectively batting about one for two in marital matters and he took shameful relief in this.

There was a slo-pitch softball league his old friends played in and they were often short of bodies. In the course of his three-week trip home he played eight games. He'd gotten fatter than he had realized in the city, and ran slower than he had expected—looking down at his feet as he trundled to first base, he'd think, What's with this? But his friends were fatter than they had been, too. Drinking together late at night, the stars improbably bright in the excessively warm prairie sky, they sweated with one another on a succession of patios and porches. Nobody talked about their marriages.

The world wears us all down. This is improbable but potent solace.

# COUNTRY OF COLD

## I

Rick "the Stick" Robinson was thrown over the top rope by the Barracuda in the last match of Maple Leaf Wrestling's last event of the year, the day after Christmas, and when he hit the announcers' collapsible plywood table the sound was like ten thousand Christmas crackers being pulled at the same instant. It echoed on and around the nearly empty Winnipeg Arena until long after the Barracuda had stopped prancing theatrically and had begun to look concerned, even climbing over the ropes in his flippers and taking off his green rubber fish mask to better see whether Rick was hurt.

Daphne stood when the action stopped, and her first instinct was to offer to help somehow, but then she saw Rick's hand rise up from the wreckage of the table and she sat down and resumed eating her popcorn. A spare microphone was located and Ralph Lazio, the announcer, resumed his breathless baritone. He emphasized to the ladies and gentlemen that Robinson *looks like he is really hurting—you can tell from the agony etched on his face* and admonished the referee for not disciplining that madman (voice deepening) the fishman, the Barra-CUDA. Daphne wondered idly where Lazio had ever heard of agony being etched on anyone's face; earlier in the afternoon, he had protested the inability of the Stryker Brothers to subscribe to even the most fundamental precepts of sportsmanlike conduct. Ernie Stryker had looked confused when he heard that; it looked like his feelings might have been hurt. The drunker Lazio was, the stranger his narration became.

As the Stick began tentatively rising from the wreckage of the table, the referee, impotent and eternally silent little grey-haired man, began wagging his finger at the Barracuda, who had replaced his fish mask by this point and was posturing again. Rick stood and made tentative and insincere motions to climb back into the ring, but the referee had disqualified the Barra-CUDA by this point and the match was Rick's anyway. Rick allowed his hand to be raised desultorily and a thin "ding" of the bell concluded the match. The Barracuda was already walking away. There was still time to get to the Boxing Day sales.

Daphne stood with the rest of the paltry audience and began to shuffle out. It was a bright and ferociously cold day. Only the genuinely committed professional wrestling fan showed up on a day like this. Ralph Lazio's amplified and effusive best wishes for the New Year trailed off in the clatter of folding chairs and Daphne made her way to the exit. Around her, men shuffled to the door, speaking quietly about the match and the home renovation projects they planned. There was a great deal of spotted plaid flannel involved and the burgundy industrial carpets that designated the walkway were stained with the muddy footprints of dozens and dozens of pairs of rubber-soled Grubers and Polartuffs.

Wrestling had undergone a resurgence of popularity since the Winnipeg Jets had moved traitorously to that hockey Mecca, Phoenix, Arizona. *Arizona*. And as wrestling came to fill the city's Saturday afternoons, even the most committed sports-entertainment fans were conscious of the decline this represented, in the city, and in them. At the wrestling matches, half the crowd wore sweatpants; everyone seemed to have gone thinner on top.

Daphne had grown up just outside the city during the hockey years, and this place now seemed to her very different from the Winnipeg she had known; her reacquaintance with the city had been complicated over these last few months by her familiarity with a more optimistic, now vanished version of this place.

Every young person she had known growing up had left the city, if they could. Their parents were often still here, however, and when she ran into them, usually at the Hudson's Bay downtown store, she spent odd minutes listening to news of her old friends. What was subsequently reported back to them, in turn, could not have been flattering, and afterwards, as she scurried to her car in the parking lot, Daphne would wince, thinking of the tenor of the next Sunday afternoon's ritual telephone call.

At the Velvet Olive sports bar, the big-screen TV was already showing the pre-game interviews before the Canadiens took the ice. The city had mostly cheered for Montreal before the advent of the Jets, and most of the hockey fans were now in the painful process of coming around again to supporting their longtime nemesis, having individually concluded that, in the end, it is necessary to root for someone or it is impossible to watch sports, or do much else. Winnipeggers had spent their fifteen golden hockey-blessed years loathing Montreal precisely because they were so good: Patrick Roy's preposterously quick hands in goal, and Guy Charboneau's resolve on the red line—these points of aggravation now turned begrudgingly into something else. Allegiance changes of this sort always cost more than expected, and for many it was too painful. Instead of watching hockey on television they went to the wrestling matches, where their hearts were less likely to be broken.

Daphne had taken to spending time at the Olive because the wrestlers hung out here. They were here

most afternoons by three, after their workouts, and, except
for Saturdays, they generally stayed here until closing.
Individual elements varied but a central core persisted,
including Rick the Stick, Barking Mad Maurice Millard,
Sultry Sally, and Stainless Steel Stan. They were probably
all alcoholics, Daphne had reflected at one point—at
several points, actually—but the context of their lives
made that a hard thing to judge. They got up at noon
and worked out until the mid-afternoon and then they
had finished their day's work. She found them entertaining and she eavesdropped on them for hours at a
stretch. This had been going on six months now. It was
like living in a motel room—it had an alarming way of
just going on. She had more money in the bank than she
could understand and whenever her bank branch man-
ager called her to talk about interest-bearing securities
she said she was sick, could she call him back?

She thought that everyone has to make such a deal
with themselves sometimes, so that they can get through
the difficulty of living. What they are doing is the pragmatic thing to do, where they are living the pragmatic
place to be. Afterwards they'll return to where they are
known and want to be and they'll resume their life as
they had left it, the only difference being that their most
pressing problem will be solved and the rest of their
problems may then be addressed at leisure.

She had begun dyeing her hair more red than she'd
intended, and buying her clothes at the thrift shop across

the street from her apartment block. Her favourite out-
fit involved a sequined leather jacket with the word
"Sparkle" spelled out across its back; there were, as well,
a number of ruffled blouses she had found in used clothing shops that pleased her, and varieties of denim pants
that spanned the fashion aesthetic. She made an impression in her bar, which is what she intended; everyone
remembered her from one day to the next, and this pro-
vided for her at least the illusion of familiarity and
acceptance. It sufficed.

That Boxing Day, Daphne studied Rick as he
entered the Velvet Olive, limping and leaning to one
side. His back, again. The paper had reported a compres-
sion fracture eight months earlier when the Belly had
mistimed a pile driver and left Rick nearly a broken
stick. This could be just a muscle pull this time, but he
was going to have to be more careful. One of these days
it was going to be a disc. She sipped her piña colada and
flipped through the newspaper, watching as he sat down
at the bar with his friends—who, like him, had never
been approached by Vince McMahon as possible foils
for his creations, and had never had even as much as a
glimpse of making enough money that you didn't have
to have roommates. And now they were all pushing
thirty and they were part-time professional wrestlers on
the Maple Leaf Wrestling circuit, one of the better-
known in western Canada, and the day after Christmas
they were drinking Molsons in the Velvet Olive, and

avoiding the looks of one of the resident weirdos, who sat in the same chair whenever she was there, which was pretty much whenever, and faced them and pretended not to be staring.

Daphne had become preoccupied by Rick the Stick over the course of a dozen Saturday afternoons that winter, watching his good-but-dull straight-guy character being pummelled into one type of submission or another by a series of mustachioed black-tighted men and at least one woman. He had sandy brown hair and cautious sideburns that seemed cultivated to evoke the idea of the congenial home appliance repairman. He was not as muscular as any of the villains, and even his briefs were modest, the dark red of a collegiate swimmer's bathing suit. He was booth-tanned and too polite for his vocation. The night he was beaten by Sultry Sally's erstwhile rival, Nikki Stryker, he had just stood there as he was tossed from corner to corner like one of the wrestling midget cousins, the Lapierres. Except that René and Jean would have struggled more than he did. Anybody would have.

After the matches, and the Velvet Olive, she would walk back through the snow to the room she had rented on the top floor of an elderly Hungarian widow's house on Sherbrooke Avenue. There she drank piña colada coolers and fantasized about her and Rick living together in a house on a leafy street. She could buy him his own little fitness centre, and he could give up professional wrestling. She imagined having a medical practice that she ran out of their living room and after he got home and she finished with her last patient, they could go watch Double A baseball out at the stadium.

When she had moved in over a year ago she had advised her landlady that she would likely only be there for a few months at the most, just as long as it took her to make some plans. Daphne had paid the rent that month and then the next and then the next after that. It had been easier to stay than she had expected. The limited space meant that she had few decisions to make about what she should buy to furnish the place. Anyway, she did not want to surround herself with clutter. She had decisions to make, and the less there was to get in the road of that, the better.

The state of in-transit reflection became, for Daphne, her dwelling place. Her mother telephoned her every week from Dunsmuir to ask what she was going to do next month. She agreed each time that it was time to make some decisions. But she soon developed sympathy for all the middle-aged unemployed unshaven men who rented rooms in her building and spoke ambitiously but imprecisely of the future.

At the bar this night wrestlers were in a good mood—most of them were headed to Mexico for a week, leaving the next day on a package tour to Mazatlán; the

travel agent was a fan of theirs and gave them a deal.
Sultry Sally was dressed as a marimba dancer and bought
a round of tequila for the table. Maurice Millard tried out
his stammering Spanish on her. She laughed and let loose
a string of Spanish invective with convincing fluidity.

The flight was leaving early the next morning and
the wrestlers had to be at the airport two hours beforehand. Bon voyages were expressed. Promises to return
with large bottles of forbidden foreign liquor were
made. They left before midnight, leaving Rick and the
Barracuda sitting there, marooned. In the sudden quiet,
the Barracuda asked again how Rick's back was. "Fine,"
Rick said.

"Do you mind me asking you a question?"

"Sure," Rick said, smiling as he sipped his Labatt
Blue.

"How much longer do you see yourself doing this?
With your back and everything?"

Rick shrugged. "Not too long, I don't think."

"Sorry about the top-rope thing."

"It was as much my doing as yours," Rick said. "I lost
my balance there and popped right over."

The Barracuda put some money on the table and
stood. "I've got a sauna in my house—if you think the
steam would help. There's a massage table too."

"I'm pretty tired," Rick said. "I'll be heading home
myself in a few minutes. Just want to see the last of this
Canadiens game."

"Okay, see you around."

Daphne watched the Barracuda leave and then she watched Rick watching the hockey game. She looked down at the wrestling schedule she had picked up at the match that afternoon. There was a cage match scheduled for January. Maurice versus "An Unidentified Menace." Midget wrestling in the first week of February. Tag team championships on Valentine's Day. Quite a year of sports entertainment shaping up.

She was startled when Rick pulled out the chair across from her at her table and sat down on it. His eyebrows were raised and he set his glass of beer down before him. "Hello," Daphne said.

"Hi. Name's Rick," Rick replied, offering his hand.

"Daphne."

"I've seen you around, haven't I?"

"Maybe."

"Maybe."

That night, at his apartment, Daphne studied the books on his shelves and the hockey posters on his walls as he poured drinks in his little kitchen. He possessed a formidable stock of alcohol. This could be interpreted as a demonstration of foresight for the Christmas season, or of anticipated excess, or both. Genuinely hard-core alcoholics rarely would have a cupboard that full, she decided—it wouldn't last long enough to accumulate. She thought about that for a while. Still, there was no denying where they had met. Where they spent most evenings every week. She wondered if she was a genuinely hard-core alcoholic. Probably even odds, at this point.

They were both partly drunk already. In the kitchen Rick was stirring away at the martinis with obvious concentration. His eyes were narrowed and, just by looking at him, she could taste his pleasure.

The apartment, for Daphne, took on the narrowed-depth-of-field focus of an arty photograph. Since she had come south, she had been imagining her life as a series of poses, stills. When Rick leaned closer to her he became blurred, and when he leaned back, even a little bit, his features merged into one another. When she leaned backward and forward, his bookshelf did like-wise. The scene had the saturated colour and weighty dialogue of a Hal Hartley film. That's it, she decided, I'm in a Hal Hartley film. What would happen next? I'll lean forward and kiss him and he'll reply with a meaning-laden non sequitur. She leaned forward and kissed him.

"Do you normally wear glasses?" he asked.

In the morning he rose before her and made scrambled eggs. There was coffee too and orange juice and toast. She sat at his little Formica table. He read the sports pages and she looked out on the tree-lined street outside his window. The skeletal bare branches swayed slowly in the wind and snow accumulated on the branches and then swept into the air. A blizzard was forming. This made his otherwise generic and slightly squalid little apartment seem cozy and self-contained, when on any other day it would feel confining. People not from northern prairie cities think them cursed by their weather, but those who know them understand that the winter is their only redemption. She wanted to curl up for the whole day there on Rick's oddly-coloured chesterfield, and watch the blowing snow. But she had already made that mistake. After breakfast, she had learned, one leaves.

In the last six months of not working she had swallowed a number of forkfuls of scrambled eggs and had left after a number of breakfasts, in a number of kitchens. She'd found the human contact tantalizing, and ultimately elusive. She read somewhere that the word "tantalize" comes from a mythical king named Tantalus, condemned forever to stand, parched, in a streambed, whose waters receded always just beyond his lips, and underneath a grape vine whose fruit withdrew similarly. Daphne kept waiting for the scrambled eggs to leap from her fork just as she opened her mouth, and that is pretty much what usually happened anyway.

So this morning at Rick's she put on her coat right after breakfast and got ready to go. He looked surprised that she was leaving already and asked her if she didn't want to stay for another cup of tea, almost as if he meant it. And she said, no, she had to go, with similar sincerity.

That night in the bar, she was reading her *People* magazine and pretending not to be watching any of the several entrances when he tipped her magazine over and grinned at her. She sat straight up, straighter than she had in fifteen months.

He sat down.

"You look well rested anyway," he said.

"How was your workout?"

"Distracted."

"Oh well."

Daphne and Rick took turns buying one another Keno tickets and drinks. When it was time to leave she asked him to come to her room. As they walked there, they spoke, in the manner of stuck people, about their ambitions. Rick had been a gymnast in university but had taken a year off when he ran short of money. "I worked for the Parks Department for a while and then it became hard to stop. I'd get laid off every October when the snow fell and every summer I made way more than enough money to get me by. The idea was that I was making up my mind about what was next, but what was always immediately next was that job. Then one day my workout partner got a job wrestling and a few weeks after that he tore his anterior cruciate ligament and he called me. Getting used to wrestling took up another three years, and here I am. Still trying to figure out what comes next, still not. It isn't anymore that I have such a long list of ambitions from which to choose."

In her room he hung his jacket on the hook on the back of her door and looked around. Out the window was the streetlight-lit blowing snow that they had just walked through. There were a few cabs in sight, making their way up Ellice Avenue, and on the sidewalk, hunched-over men stumbled in the snow. The wind blew a little harder and her window rattled. He sat down on her bed, without being asked. He looked at her and lifted his eyebrows.

"I was a family doctor up north until a year ago," she said.

He nodded.

"I mishandled a difficult situation. It was a catastrophe."

"Did you get charged with something?"

She blinked. "You mean, by the police?"

He nodded. She shook her head. "It doesn't work like that with these things. Unless there's a pattern of it, or you were drunk, you just go away, generally. If you can put it out of your own mind, maybe no one ever mentions it to you again."

"So what are you going to do?"

"What I'm doing."

"Which is?"

And she kissed him.


Over breakfast the next morning, at the Harmon's Drugs lunch counter, he poked at his over-easy eggs with a piece of whole wheat toast until the yolk was liberated and he could soak it up. The little packages of marmalade beside his plate sat unused. It was just after noon and they were still waking up. The frozen stumble-dash to the diner had not waked them so much as added another layer of confused sensation to their bodies. Daphne drank her coffee and watched the waitresses bustle. She was happy. When she was happy, she remembered, she spoke more directly.

"This business of waiting for yourself to get on with things is funny. It's like, if you know you have to, then what is the obstacle?"

He was still in his clothes from the night before, and smelled of cigarette smoke from the bar, and his hair was in disarray. He was markedly unshaven, and in the winter afternoon's thin light, among the room full of hungover university students and socializing senior citizens, she thought to herself that she could sit here and prattle on to him forever.

He chewed his yolk-sodden toast for a moment and then swallowed. Gesticulating with the little triangular toast remnant in his hand, he replied, "I understand that this is just a little exercise in vanity, my life, the way it is now, the wrestling. But I look at the community college course calendar every now and then, and I just can't picture being that guy, that welder, or refrigeration systems technician. I wonder, where is the greatness in that? We are what we do. Job-jobs like that terrify me."

Their waitress, Evelyn smiley face, came by to refill their coffees. Rick smiled back at her. She asked if there was anything else they wanted. He looked at Daphne. She shook her head. Evelyn nodded and left the bill at the table. "*People* magazine does this to us," he said. "We think that average is way below acceptable. Average is average. It's normal. Being normal is healthy, or it always used to be. When we assume our lives to be in some way special, we load up our troubles with all this horsepower they aren't really entitled to. I've been reading about that in this book, *Know and Set Your Limits: A Guide to Business Strategy in the New Economy*, have you read it?"

She shook her head no.

"The author teaches at the Stanford Business School, and climbs icefalls in his spare time, the jacket says. He seems to understand people pretty well."

"I'll have to get it from the library."

"You can read my copy when I'm done with it."

"Well hurry up and finish it then."

"Don't rush me, man."

"Gimme a kiss."

"Say please."

"Gimme."

"Gimme gimme never gets."

Evelyn was standing beside the table with a coffeepot in her hand. She rolled her eyes and hoisted it with her eyebrows raised. They shook their heads in unison, mouths slightly agape. Evelyn walked off.

Daphne put her head on the table and covered it. "Whatever happened to my brain?" she asked, from within. She sounded like she was under a pile of clothing and her words came out almost unintelligible. She looked up at him. He patted her head and returned to the hockey pages of the paper. She watched him. She thought to herself that there it was, she was going to be okay now. Whichever way things went from here, she wasn't entirely broken.

After another half hour of remarkably slow sports page reading, she counted out the money for the bill and stood. He reached for her coat and handed it to her. She put on her toque. He put on his. As they left the drugstore he wrapped her scarf around her.

The following weekend, at the indoor driving range, she finally took the bait: "I know what you're saying and I know you like that book you're reading, but it's pretty hard to imagine not taking your own life pretty seriously." She swung the driver as hard as she could and hit the ball squarely, watching it rise to the net. It was a good hit. She hated golf, but was discovering how much she liked hitting that little ball.

"Yeah, it is. But if we understood ourselves to be just exactly as important as we are, then we would save ourselves a lot of grief. That wouldn't be not taking your life seriously, it would be seeing it realistically. And doing the job that you're supposed to do. Like this book says . . ."

"Please don't quote that book to me."

He looked up. "Okay."

"We have different problems, I think."

"I think they're the same problem. You are unable to conceive of anything but the obit version of your life—noble and self-sacrificing, uncomplicated by scandal or error. Me, I can't come up with even that, for myself. But really, it's the same problem."

She hit the ball again. It flew straight to the end of the range and hit the net, still rising. She placed another ball quickly on the carpet in front of her and readied her driver, adjusting her grip. She realized that he was suddenly irritating her; she resented being reduced to an aphorism. She found her stance and swung the club back very far. She looked at his satisfied face and disliked how pleased he was with his phrase "obit version of your life." No doubt it was a chapter subtitle in that book he was reading. She struck the ball hard, so hard that everyone nearby turned to glance at the crack and her own involuntary grunt. The ball sailed off to the end of the range; she lost sight of it long before it approached the net. She turned to him, her face set. "Your turn."

He sensed the change in her mood and that he had been talking too much. He hit balls for a while and then handed the club back to her. In the clatter and whirr of flying golf balls there was almost no speech, as there was now no speech between Daphne and Rick. She finished off the bucket and said she had to go home, she had things to do. This was only a week after they had eaten breakfast together at Harmon's Drugs.

She did not go to the Olive that night, as she had promised. She stayed home and the next morning she slept late, as was her custom, and when it was time for her to get up she rolled over again and shut her eyes. She kept on doing that until she heard the hum of the drive-home traffic in the street. Then she listened to the radio beside her bed until it was dark out.

She showered quickly in the washroom at the end of the hall and dressed there too. She pulled on her clothes and went outside. She was hungry, and walked down to the McDonald's on Portage Avenue, where she ordered a Big Mac and fries, and a Coke. She wrote a note as she ate. Then she put on her coat and walked over to Rick's apartment. She slipped it under the door. His apartment caretaker saw her do this and they exchanged frowns.

The note had her phone number on it and asked him to call her, and said that she didn't want to go to the Velvet Olive.

He met her at the Harmon's Drugs lunch counter the next afternoon. "Is anything the matter?" he asked.

"Here's the deal," she said. "We're both losers. Everyone who works with us thinks this. Our parents suspect it, and so do we. Neither one of us is great. And when you tell me that we are, *I am*, what I do, then what you are telling me is that I am nothing. Because I am doing nothing. And actually, I've noticed that."

"Whoa."

"Whoa what?"

"Honey, you're not a loser, and . . ."

"*Honey, I am*, and it's okay, and you are too, and that's okay. Just don't rationalize it for me anymore, okay?"

"I won't think of myself like that, even if you have to, for some reason."

"Okay. In any event, maybe it is time to stop doing nothing. I've been thinking about getting work here and moving into a proper house or something, maybe down on Wolseley Avenue."

"That's a great idea."

"Yeah, well, it's about time anyway. I don't want to philosophize anymore about all this. I just want to do this, and go forward, okay?"

"Sure," he said, leaning back.

"Good." She exhaled.

"I'm not sure why you needed me to come down here and hear this, though."

She stared at him blankly.

"I mean, after all, what you do is your business, and what I do is mine."

She kept staring.

"And if you don't like how I see the world moving forward, then fine."

She blinked. He stood up. She couldn't think of what she should say. She had gotten way ahead of herself, but she thought also that this was the last chance she had to be absurd without being ridiculous. She couldn't think of what to say.

"See you around," he said, and left.

Three months later, near the end of March, she ran into him at the Bay. It was a sunny day and the snow was melting quickly. Spring had come in the course of an afternoon two days earlier and it had turned abruptly from too cold to intoxicatingly warm. In the air one could smell damp and mouldy grass for the first time in half a year. The whole city was happy and walking down the sand-covered sidewalks with their parkas unzipped smiling like they were deranged. She spotted him in the luggage department. "Going on a trip?" she asked, as she sidled up to him, perusing a rack of the less expensive canvas-sided models.

"Hey," he said. "There you are."

"Yep."

"I haven't seen you around anywhere."

She shrugged. "Where are you going?"

"Pittsburgh."

"Why?"

"Mr. McMahon's office gave me a call the other day."

"No way."

"Scout's honor."

"Whoa."

"It's maybe just a temporary thing—someone on his circuit blew their knee out."

"How's your back?" she asked.

"Much better. Or, anyway, better enough."

"So when are you going?"

"In a few days. I have to move out of my apartment here and take care of some things."

"Wow. This is so great. What's your handle going to be?"

"I dunno. They didn't think much of 'Rick the Stick.' I think they just tell me what it'll be."

"That's probably best."

"Yes."

"So I won't hold you up then. You're probably swamped with things to do before you go."

"It's pretty busy, yes."

"So, listen, best of luck," and she stuck out her hand.

"Best of luck," he repeated distractedly, shaking her hand.

"I'm gonna go," she said.

"Me too," he said.

"I'm working again, now."

"I know."

"You know?"

"That's what you said you were going to do when we last talked."

"Right, but I actually did it."

"I thought you would."

"You *did*?"

"Yeah. I mean, why not? It was time, wasn't it?"

"It seems it was."

"I'm gonna go," he said.

"Yes. You should give me a call sometime."

"Sure. These days are pretty busy, but I will when I have a chance."

"I moved."

"Do you have a pen?"

"No."

"Me either."

"It's listed."

"Okay."


## II


A year and a half ago she had been fly-fishing in the Partridge River when the snow had started falling, early September and hardly a surprise. She had caught three char in the space of a couple of hours and so perhaps she hadn't watched the sky as closely as she ought to have. By the time she had her gear loaded up on her ATV and was headed back to town, the tundra was already disappearing beneath the snow.

An old story, and one she had heard about a dozen times in the two years she'd been up there, about how quickly the weather changes in the early autumn and how Kablunauks all think it feels far too much like summer to blizzard—but it does and in an instant the bright and exquisite summer tundra disappears and that is it, winter is there and nothing halfway about it.

But by the time she had gone a couple hundred yards she knew she was in trouble. She had been off the trail for a least a few minutes when she finally acknowledged that she couldn't see a thing. She brought the ATV to a stop, shuddering with fear as she let it idle and looked around, into the wind and the snow. She had a tarp, and a warm coat. She called the nursing station on her VHF. She was barely able to make out a reply. They were barely able to make out her. It didn't matter. One look out the window would tell them what the trouble was.

She pulled the tarp up over the ATV on one side and weighted down the edge with rocks. It made a sort of lean-to and she pulled in her pack and her gear with her. She was out of the wind, at least, which is a very big deal in circumstances such as these. Her idea was to stay awake and warm by doing abdominal crunches beneath the tarp.

She got to 250 when she fell back, exhausted. That would keep her going for at least a little while, she figured.

When she awoke it was early morning and the sky was quiet. She wasn't sure why she had awoken; what she had always been told was that if one fell asleep in the snow, one simply became colder and colder until one's heart stopped. She was very stiff. She was too cold to shiver. It was as if her body had known the trouble she was in and stirred her one last time. The wind had stopped. When she crawled out from under her lean-to and stood up, the sun was glowing orange against the sparkling plane of snow all around her.

It took her a few minutes to get the ATV going, but when it coughed into life she finally exhaled. She loaded her gear back on and revved the engine. She wasn't sure exactly where she was and the land looked very different under the snow. She drove slowly in the direction she had been headed when she stopped. She came to a stream she didn't recognize, and realized that she was headed upstream, inland and away from town. She turned around and followed the current of the stream. After twenty minutes it met the Tagak River, which she knew. Another two hours after that she saw the lights of the airport on the horizon. She followed them into town. The ATV belonged to the nursing station, and so she drove there and put it away in the garage. The station was lit up, she noticed, and she walked to the door.

Inside was bedlam. Dozens of people had been out fishing when the storm hit and most were still on the land. All the nurses had been called in and were attending a stream of mild frostbite and hypothermia. Mary, one of the long-timers, noticed Daphne and nodded to her. She nodded back.

"You okay?" she asked.

"Yeah. How are things around here?"

"Lotsa little stuff. The people who've come in so far mostly weren't out there long enough to get into trouble. A lot of folks still on the land, though."

"How many do you think?"

"Nobody is sure, exactly."

"Kablunauks?"

"Including you, only a couple, as far as we know."

"The locals will probably be okay."

"Probably, except for the teenagers."

Daphne showered there, at the nursing station, and put her char into the freezer in the lunchroom. She thought to herself that it was time to take an actual holiday, get to Cuba or something.

Sarah was eight and her brother Robert nine. They had been out hunting with their uncle Lukie Oktuk when the snow started falling. They were much farther out than Daphne had been, fifty miles up the Meliadine River, and there was no thought given to travelling in that weather. Lukie Oktuk pitched his tent and blocked the wind with their ATV. Then he shovelled snow around the tent and they all crawled inside. He stepped outside to light a lamp, and when he came back into the tent the warm orange light of the lamp set aside any gnawing worry the three of them might have had.

They each took off their boots and then crawled into their sleeping bags. Lukie told his niece and nephew a bedtime story about *Indiana Jones and the Temple of Doom.*

(They all remembered with their mind's eye, the scene being evoked—they had watched the video together two weeks ago: Harrison Ford panting gamely as he swings from jungle vine to jungle vine; who could imagine a place actually like that, what would it smell like?) When the stone goblins had all been decapitated, Lukie turned the lamp low and they all went to sleep. The wind was howling outside and the nylon fabric of the tent shivered with each gust.

The lamp went out sometime in the course of the evening, and with it out, the tent became cold very quickly. Robert was the first to awake, and he crawled out of his sleeping bag and took the lamp down off the hook Lukie had hung it from. He opened the fuel cap and found the fuel bottle Lukie had set beside the tent door. He filled the lamp carefully and replaced the cap. He lit a match and touched it to the wick. The wick flared brightly and he turned it down.

The tent was abruptly colder, not warmer, Robert noticed, and he looked away from the bright flame of the lamp to see how this could be. The walls of the tent were peeling back like tissue paper. Drops of burning nylon splattered down on the tent floor, and all three sleeping bags were alight. Sarah was screaming and Lukie awoke, looked around twice, and stood, his hair catching fire as it brushed the tent. He put his arms into Sarah's burning sleeping bag and pulled her out; he swung her into the crook of his left arm and his right arm caught Robert by the waist. They charged out of the tent and into the snow. Lukie pushed Sarah face-down into the snow and rolled her in it. Then he did the same to Robert.

In the night Robert, Sarah, and Lukie watched the tent burn down as they stood in the tundra in their underwear. The fire was finished in minutes. They approached the tent when it had died down and tried to find something to wear. The sleeping bags were mats of partially melted and burned feathers. The boots were all destroyed too; there were a total of three mittens that could still be worn, and Lukie put two on Sarah and one on Robert. The rifle was undamaged, in its hard plastic case, and the ammunition had not exploded.

Lukie started up the ATV, which had not caught fire. He put the rifle in the komatik and put Robert in the front of the seat and Sarah between them. He drove to the river ford where the caribou had been crossing for the last three days. The caribou were bedded down, and as the ATV approached, the more nervous females lifted their heads and lowed. There were dozens of them visible, even in the thin moonlight. That year's calves huddled under the snow close to their mothers. Lukie drove to within a hundred yards of one cluster of animals. Then he stopped the ATV and opened the rifle case.

He dropped most of the shells he tried to feed into the magazine, his fingers were so numb by this point. He rested the rifle against the seat of the ATV and aimed for the largest animal. He fired. He lifted his head and rotated the bolt of the rifle, drawing it back and sliding it forward. He lowered his head and fired again. The caribou rose to their feet, looking around confusedly in all directions. He fired again. Three animals remained standing as the others trotted slowly away. They all coughed repeatedly. One lowered her head and appeared to vomit, then slumped onto her forelegs, kneeling, and then lying. The other two walked around in small circles before collapsing. Lukie drove the ATV over to the dead caribou and skinned them quickly. The bodies, ungutted and otherwise whole, lay like pink anatomic models in the snow as Lukie wrapped Sarah and Robert in the still bloody and glistening hides, before wrapping one around himself.

He turned the ATV downriver and drove as fast as he could. He could feel Sarah shivering between his legs and he crouched over her as completely as he could. By the time he could see the lights of the airport on the horizon she had stopped shivering.

When Daphne was called to the treatment room, she was still towelling herself off. Her first thought was that she was sure it could wait until she put on some clothes, for crying in the sink. When the janitor pounded on the door of the shower again, she pulled her sweatshirt over her shoulders and stepped into a pair of sweatpants. She looked out into the hall and he was standing there, bouncing up and down in little steps. He waved her down the hall.

Sarah was lying on the treatment-room cot. She was whimpering quietly and would not open her eyes. The nurses were getting IVs started and someone had measured her temperature at twenty-nine degrees Celsius, profoundly hypothermic. She had a blood pressure, though, and she was already on a monitor. Her pulse was 160.

Daphne's first thought was that things could not possibly be as bad as they looked. The girl's face was a waxen sheet of third-degree burns, interspersed by charred clothing and hair. She was gasping for air. Her burned and blood-covered brother and uncle were standing in one corner, huddled together, aghast.

Daphne started an IV line in the child's groin. She listened to her lungs with a stethoscope. There wasn't much air moving in her skinny and burned little chest. She blinked away tears. She looked in her mouth. Sarah's tongue and palate were crimson and swollen. She had not completely obstructed. It would be very difficult to get an endotracheal tube into her trachea with all that swelling. She put an oxygen mask on her and hoped that the swelling would settle down. A nurse pulled a bag of warmed saline from the microwave oven and connected it to a rectal tube. She placed the tube and began running the warm saline in. She placed a hot-air warming blanket on the little girl. Someone remeasured her core temperature and it was thirty degrees.

Around the child: madness. Three nurses, Daphne, an RCMP officer, and the janitor all yelling at the same time about what they think should be done, what they can offer. The janitor wants to know if he should call the airport and initiate a medevac. The nurses think that they need more IVs. They do. This was the worst thing Daphne had ever seen. She couldn't think clearly, could barely even breathe herself, really, and she just wanted the child to breathe, dammit, *breathe*.

They always say that it never hurts to hope, but when things need to be done, problems need to be reckoned with, hope paralyzes. It feels like it is an action itself, that the act of hoping addresses the need for hope itself, some-how. But it isn't so, it isn't ever so, and it wasn't so now.

When Daphne leaned back, hoping that the child would start breathing, hoping that she wouldn't have to try to get a tube into her lungs, she knew she was not handling this as she should. So it was less of a surprise to her than it would otherwise have been when things became abruptly worse and the child stopped breathing.

She reached for the laryngoscope that one of the nurses had been waving at her for the last several min-utes. She lifted Sarah's tongue up and to the side with it and tried to catch a glimpse of her vocal cords. The nor-mal anatomic architecture was so distorted she could not even begin to guess what she was looking at. There was nothing that looked like vocal cords. There wasn't a passage of any sort that looked like it would allow the tube to pass. All she saw was hamburger, initially scarlet but now increasingly blue. She pulled the laryngoscope out and asked for the Melkor set, the kit that was supposed to allow one to surgically place a tube through the skin in front of the throat, in situations like this. There was some fussing and searching while this was found and Sarah grew bluer and bluer and her heart rate began to slow. Finally it was dumped on the child's chest in front of Daphne and she slapped a little iodine down on her neck and felt for her Adam's apple. All she could feel was thickened burned skin. She pushed the needle in approximately where she thought she should be. She got air. She cut the skin and pushed in the guide and then the tracheostomy tube. Her heart rate was thirty-five. She was as blue as a plum. Daphne pumped air in and out of the tube with the resuscitation bag. It wouldn't go.

She remembered her physiology professor lecturing her class that humans are like seals, and we can descend beneath the surface and survive on stored oxygen for a time. But, like seals, when it is time to ascend, and breathe fresh air, then we must, and if we do not, then our muscles weaken and the ability to ascend is lost. Every living thing understands the idea of living on stored resources, cached fuel and food; marriages continue on the basis of previously established goodwill, and men with runs of bad luck and eroding ambition pawn their tools to pay the motel bill, and even the idea of living on the principal sends shudders into every accountant's marrow. These are survivable if undesirable predicaments, for a time, right up until the moment when they aren't, and the ability to reascend is lost.

She looked at the child's chest again. The burned and swollen skin was rising off her rib cage like a caterpillar egg case on a twig. Daphne grabbed the scalpel from the Melkor kit and made an incision from each armpit to her hip, to allow the rib cage to expand, free of the constricting effect of that thickened and swollen skin. It was possible to bag-ventilate her now. But her heart rate had fallen to twenty. Pink froth came up the breathing tube into the bag. Her heart stopped.

When Sarah's mother arrived she walked straight into the resuscitation room and was not addressed. No one could make eye contact with her. She stood at the doorway and looked at her little daughter, motionless and blue, on the stretcher, no one standing close to her, no one doing anything to her anymore. The nurses looked at Daphne, who approached the child's mother haltingly. Robert ran past her and up to his mother, seizing her around the waist. Lukie would not look at his sister, could not even face her, and turned away from her and toward the wall, his hands over his ears, crouching.

In the treatment of thermal injuries associated with oro-labial inflammation, it is imperative to secure

airway protection with immediate endotracheal intubation, as progressive swelling of the glottic structures
is usual, and subsequently renders intubation more
difficult or, indeed, impossible.

—*Emergency Therapeutics,* K. Zbuk,

p. 234, Edmonton, 1994


The essential tactic necessary for successful treatment of severe burn injuries is the anticipation and
treating of complications before they become life
threatening—escharotomies may be performed on
the chest before respiratory embarrassment occurs
and airway protection and volume infusion need to
be performed before clinical evidence of obstruc-
tion and dehydration become manifest. Severe burns
kill very quickly and their complications progress
with extraordinary rapidity; these complications are
predictable but they progress so fast that they are,
essentially, only treatable when they are as yet un-
expressed.

—*Management of the Trauma Patient,* D. Woodley,

p. 118, Regina, 1978


In reviewing the management of this patient, it is
determined that frank malpractice was not a feature,
although several suggestions may be made to the
practitioner regarding ways in which her care might
be optimized. In particular, some remedial training

in airway management may be contemplated, if she is to continue to provide emergency care of the critically ill. . . .

—*Proceedings of the Disciplinary Committee of*
*the College of Physicians of the Northwest Territories,*
pp. 23–27, May 1997

Lukie came to see Daphne in her office two weeks later. That morning when she started work she saw his name on the appointment book and all the rest of the morning she had been thinking about what he wanted, how he was doing. She had spent the previous two weeks trying hard not to think about Sarah. In her dreams, she saw dogs eating the child as she fought, and Daphne stood by, wondering why the dogs found her so appetizing. She awoke often in the middle of the night sobbing; her neighbours around her all knew of the events of that evening. The men looked at her sympathetically, the women mostly could not meet her eyes.

When Lukie was led into her office she had no idea what to say. Though his burns were healing, he looked awful. His posture was stooped and his skin grey; he smelled bad and had evidently not washed or shaved since the accident.

"Mr. Oktuk, how are you doing?" she asked, after she had closed the door and sat back down. He looked at the floor, and then out her window.

"Not that well, I guess. You?"

"Been better."

"Yeah."

"Your burns look like they're coming along."

"They're okay. They don't bother me much."

"How is your sister?"

"She is very sad."

"Do you have any questions about what happened that day?"

"I heard that she didn't have to die."

"From who?"

"Someone who knows one of the nurses."

"I could have done things differently when she got here. If I had the chance to do it over again, there are things I would do differently."

He nodded. Still looking out the window. "Me too."

"Yes."

"I never thought either of them would get up and light the lamp on their own."

"Of course not."

"And they've never seen me fill a lamp inside the tent."

"I'm sure they haven't."

"I try saying that to my sister and she just looks at me like she hates me."

"She is going through some very difficult emotions right now."

"Have you talked to her?"

"She doesn't want to talk to me."

"Yeah."

Ed McFarland called Daphne to tell her that Lukie Oktuk had been found dead in his bathtub with his .30–06 between his legs. They needed blood samples for the coroner's investigation and would she come and draw them?

She found the house easily, as the police truck was parked outside with the lights flashing, visible throughout the entire town. The house itself was old and very small, painted white and peeling yellow. Tiny windows and a roof littered with antlers. There was a porch stacked with caribou hides, and a polar bear hide was nailed to the wall. Everywhere around her there was bone and frozen flesh. Inside there were three RCMP officers and another half-dozen people who acted involved, mostly standing around and nodding gravely. There was no family, though—they had all been asked to stay with relatives for the time being.

Lukie lay in the tub with the rifle in that portion of his mouth that remained. The right side of his face had been sprayed over the wall like red stucco. The left side of his face was still present, but ballooned out like a comic-book drawing, from the bullet's shock wave. The eyeball bulged as if with horror at the rest of the body's circumstances, and the profile seemed overall to suggest apoplectic horror. Daphne chewed on her mitten for a second and then she kneeled down on the plastic sheeting that had been laid over the floor. She opened her bag to extract a syringe but she couldn't find it for her tears. She kept groping in the bag for a likely-feeling object but everything felt the same and not at all like what she was looking for. She wiped her eyes for a long time and then when she opened them again they were clear. She found a twenty-millilitre syringe and an eighteen-gauge needle. She put the needle into his heart and tried to draw blood, but none came. His heart had emptied itself into the bathtub. She tried his groin, looking for the femoral vein, but nothing came. Lukie's cold waxen flesh had drained like a bled steer. She put the needle into his intact eye and drew out the acqueous humour. It would suffice. Lukie looked less animated now and less human, his eye withered like a fig. She closed his lid over it.

### III

Daphne and her two friends were sitting around a blanket, wearing cat's-eye sunglasses and sleeveless cotton blouses and skirts. Arms streaked white and pink like dispensed peppermint toothpaste. On the blanket: a Tupperware container of potato salad, a loaf of French bread, and a can of smoked oysters. A Discman with little speakers, sounding strained. The three women were looking out at the water and squinting. Daphne smoked a cigarette and looked at the horizon. She was as pale as a Noxzema Girl. She had slathered SPF ten thousand on so thick little pools of coconut-scented lotion were collecting in the sand beneath her elbows, the odour wafting upward with all the sweetness of the South Pacific. On the hairs of her upper lip, small beads of perspiration glistened and stung. In the heat, her cheeks were reddened. She put the cigarette out in the sand and blew out the last of the smoke. She took off her sunglasses for a moment and wiped her forehead. The other two remained still.

Hannah said, "I've got to get out of here. November by the latest. I can't spend another winter that depressed, that bored." She put her sunglasses on again and leaned forward, hugging her knees, adopting the same position as her friends.

Laurel said, "Summer is so great, though, that it fakes you out. It makes you think, What was I whining about again? and then winter hits and you can't move for another eight months and you're stuck in that dreadful little city." A seagull picked through a garbage bag that had washed up on the shore. It found a disposable diaper within and began extracting it optimistically.

Hannah: "Appalling." The seagull's activity had caught the attention of its brethren and a circle of gulls appeared overhead, calling loudly. "And minuscule," she added.

Laurel: "You can't even become a big fish in a small pond. There isn't enough plankton to get any bigger than anything else." They all watched the seagulls.

"That's what fish eat: plankton, right?"

"I think so," Daphne said.

"The small ones anyway," Hannah said.

"How about whales?" Laurel asked.

"They're not fish," Daphne said.

"But they eat plankton, and they're big."

"True," Daphne said.

Hannah: "And there are whale sharks; they're fish, they're big, *and* they eat plankton."

Daphne, still staring at the horizon: "I think we can agree that plankton serves as the nutritional underpinning of the whole aquatic food chain."

Laurel, to Hannah: "But I take your point, that not all fish eat plankton directly."

Hannah: "Sure."

Laurel, like anyone, hated being corrected.

The lake was the eighth-largest body of fresh water anywhere in the world. This fact surprised everyone when they learned it. It wasn't a place that presented its grandeur in any way that was obvious. In the summer, only a few weeks after the last of the snow had gone, and even while there was still ice floating in the northern basin of the lake, columns of tent trailers began their migration out to the southern end, where the beaches and ice cream stands were. For hundreds of miles, white sand stretched on between the trees and the water; it was only the surface tensions of sex and parental concern that kept the glistening mass of sun-lotioned humanity together. There were no boundaries to confine the blankets, and the sand stretched on either side into distant sharpened points. It was an astonishing place, and for all the regrettable fashion decisions and aesthetic failings, the scale of the forest and the lake still dwarfed the beet-faced people at its southern tip.

The lake bottom sloped out so gradually that some places, even a mile offshore, after swimming for an hour among whitecaps and dark green water, you could still stick your feet down and feel the bottom. What could be more reassuring than that to someone starting to tire? Or less satisfying to someone who wasn't?

In the centre of the southern basin, maybe 150 miles north of the beach towns, were islands of perfect white silica that was shipped south to be used for glassmaking. Nobody lived there. Elk Island, Bear Island, Black Island. Just the shiny white poplar trees, the sand, the eponymous animals, and clean fresh water on every side. Nobody noticed this. Sometime in the seventies *Playboy* magazine supposedly named these as one of the ten best beach spots in North America to, who knows, make the piece seem more exhaustive maybe, and the people from the city out here recited this fact to each other like a mantra.

"Here, have some more potato salad, it's my mother's recipe, it's the one thing she excelled at, poor thing, and it had to be potato salad, but there you go, God lives in the details." Daphne opened one of the Tupperware containers and began scooping out yellow lumpen potato salad onto paper plates.

Her companions sat on adjacent corners of their blanket, knees against their chests, still looking at the water. Daphne and Hannah had renewed their high school friendship three months ago. They had lost track of one another since leaving the Dairy Queen they had worked at, and upon meeting at a bar that winter they had sat and talked as if they were sisters.

Laurel had gone out with Hannah's brother until ten baleful months ago and had emerged with a new close friend in Hannah, the one acquaintance she couldn't wail on endlessly to. Dignity being the first casualty of these things. Dignity mattering.

Daphne squinted her eyes and scratched her nose. "I have to start doing something differently too. I'm miserable most of the time these days. I go to work, get my hair cut, go to movies. I feel completely frivolous."

A few months before her old sort-of-boyfriend (as she titled him in her mind) Rick left the city to make his way in the WWF, Daphne had started working in a series of walk-in clinics. She made half the money she had been making in the north, but she was less exhausted now than she was then, or indeed than she was when she wasn't working at all. She had been south for over two years now. She still thought about the people she knew in Wager Bay every day. And she was a little surprised at herself for not having gone back. But she wouldn't, and now she knew that.

She'd met Greg, her new sort-of-boyfriend, at a news-stand on Portage Avenue. He had his daughter with him and he kept looking at Daphne as his daughter merrily read aloud a Pokémon comic book. That was the only glimpse she'd had of his daughter. She had expressed a desire to meet her but Greg had never responded. Okay, Daphne thought, loud and clear. In the meantime, they met on the weekends and had sex. He was a divorced high school chemistry teacher. He brought exams over with him sometimes and sat at her kitchen table marking them as Daphne cooked supper afterwards. He was a vegetarian, and had a delicate stomach—no spices, nothing smoked or pickled. They never really got into things, ever. They found this little ritual of sex and supper the third time they saw each other and had remained in it since. It felt like they had been doing it for years. In a sense, they had. And would continue to, barring surprises.

"I know exactly what you mean," Laurel said.

"*I* don't feel frivolous," Hannah declared.

"Look at us," Laurel said. "We're the smartest and most interesting people we know. This self-questioning comes from within, it's part of our neurosis, our intelligence, maybe. You crave meaning so strongly, it's what pushes us on past our mediocrity."

She took a drag on her cigarette; Hannah nodded at the horizon.

"We are too mediocre," said Daphne. "We just have a particular taste and consider that some sort of accomplishment. None of us do that much. I don't, anyway."

The lake exists as two large basins. The southern, accessible one is 15,000 square miles and the northern one 28,000 square miles. For years, the lake was the only transportation link between the northern prairie and the outside world. Goods came down through the Arctic Sea to the tip of Hudson Bay, where they were loaded onto boats that crawled upstream to the tip of the lake, then three hundred miles along the rocky forested shore, and down the Red River to civilization. Some of the boats would turn west from the northern basin to follow the Saskatchewan River into the heart of the prairie, and it was by this means that the Canadian prairie was supplied with shaving soap and shoe polish for most of a hundred years—this was when Hudson Bay was the source of something other than ice and dread.

The lake has the history, and the scale, but it has never become, is never referred to as, a great lake, upper- or lowercase. Great Slave Lake has been deemed so from its nomination, Great Bear Lake, all the Ontario-Superior chain; who hasn't heard of Titicaca, or Baikal, or Great Salt Lake, Victoria, Malawi, the Aral Sea? All the most important lakes become adjectival phrases with com-

fortable grace: mysterious Loch Ness; Lake Victoria—
headwaters of the Nile; Baikal, the Siberian Inland Sea.
This one is too shallow, too muddy, look at all this *algae*
everywhere. The sand is dirty with pine needles, bits of
clay. It is what is available.

To the northwest, Hannah noticed a line of grey cloud
had been building up on itself for the past hour, like a
carpet wrinkling under a door edge, and now was
flattening out, and scudding its way across the sky, right
at them.

One of Hannah's favourite devices in conversation
was to lean back and say, "What do you mean?" It could
be quite disconcerting, especially if you had no idea, or
were saying something stupid. It lent discussions with
her a necessary precision, a sense of her really listening.
The effect could be quite flattering. At parties she used
this trick rather a lot and so was considered very intelligent by the other music people she knew. And she was.
The thing is, they thought that she was maybe even
smarter than *them*.

Hannah said once, with a roll of her eyes, "Musicians
always think themselves wonderfully well-spoken and
full of intelligent things to say, over and over again."
That she had this much disdain for the members of her
chosen profession belied the lack of acknowledgment,
the paucity of work she got, and no retort was sharp
enough ever to quite puncture the hissed suggestion that

she was simply resentful, and envious. The suggestion was made fairly regularly—she could tell when it was welling up even as she turned from a witticism and walked over to other people she knew. Behind her: nodding.

Hannah lived in any given period on less money than Daphne spent on restaurant meals. She bought her vegetables at the roadstands on the Perimeter Highway and bicycled great bags of them home, swerving onto the shoulder when semi-trailers passed, and leaped at house-sitting situations that involved no rent. It was a little inconceivable that someone could spend as little money as she did and still live in a city. The only thing she owned worth more than a hundred dollars was her French horn. Her clothes had many fashionable patches on them. Her brother constantly offered her money but she declined, reflexively.

When Hannah's brother and Laurel had begun their on-again-off-again-and-again-and-again breakup, Hannah had been kinder to Laurel than seemed plausible. Laurel took two weeks off from the university library where she worked, pleading pneumonia. She had been on the point of quitting entirely when Hannah compelled her to get dressed one morning and go in, accompanying her all the way and advising her to cough a bit as she went.

The extent of Hannah's kindness had seemed in itself almost a criticism of her brother's behaviour, and that was how everyone had interpreted it but him. Hannah continued to eat supper with each of them separately and never said anything about one to the other. "Shuttle diplomacy" was how Daphne had described it. "You have no idea how exhausting it is," Hannah had said.

For a few people, the lake is still essential. In the winters an ice road is created for five months, along the eastern shore of the lake. Semi-trailer trucks crawl up this road all winter long to the communities on this side of the lake. It is three hundred miles long, and is formed by phalanxes of snowplows and Caterpillar tractors that set off every December to build and mark the road. The towns it services, mostly Indian reservations, have no other land link, and so they get their fuel and heavy stores only when the ice is hard enough to carry freight. In the summer the only transportation in or out is the float planes, and the women spend their afternoons drawing up their orders for the winter freight shipment. How many hundred-pound sacks of flour and sugar, how many cans of tea and gallons of molasses and buckets of sweet clover honey, and coffee and five-pound bags of cinnamon and nutmeg. When the freeze-up is late or incomplete, families here check off every day on the calendar and pray for cold, waiting for the road to be opened. Every few years, pushing it, a truck goes through the ice.

Hannah and Laurel took ecstasy together when they were out dancing one Friday night in the winter. They were unable to agree later whose idea it had been. They ended up in a diner in an industrial park, giggling and playing with their condiment bottles. Beside the diner was a lot that the city used as a snow dump. It was late in the season and the snow reached sixty feet in the air, a great glittering bulge into the night sky that caught Laurel's attention first, and soon they were running toward it, screaming with laughter, their oilcloth placemats tucked around their coats to serve as ersatz Krazy Karpets.

They had to climb over the chain-link fence the city had erected around the hill, festooned with No Tobogganing signs. When they reached the snow pile they were awed at the size of it, thousands and thousands of tons of snow and sand and salt created since Thanksgiving. Here and there a Christmas tree stuck out, little bits of metal foil glittering under the night sky. It was overcast and just a little bit of snow was falling and the low clouds glowed yellow from the sodium lights along the roads of the industrial park.

They were halfway up the hill, snow melting in their shoes, and their faces streaked with tears from laughing so hard, when a police car pulled into the lot. A spotlight probed out into the night, lighting up a narrow cone of snowflakes between the hill and the car. Hannah and Laurel froze, and then scrambled into a little hollow in the mound. The light darted toward them and probed a few inches over and all around them. "He must have seen us moving," Hannah said.

"Shhh," Laurel said.

They lay there a long time, many minutes, until their pants were thoroughly wet from the melting snow beneath them. Hannah lifted her head to see if the car was still there. The searchlight stabbed the snow all around them again. Hannah dropped her head like a ground squirrel. They heard a car door slam.

"What're we gonna do?" Laurel asked.

"Just stay still."

"We could run for it."

"Don't be silly."

"Do you think he saw us?"

"Yes."

"Are you as scared as I am?"

"Yes."

A nasal voice called up to them, "Okay, I want you two down here right now!"

Both women jerked as if they'd been poked. Neither had been in trouble with authority since primary school, if then. They didn't move.

"All right, you bastards, let's MOOVE!"

Each woman could feel the other beside her, tetanically rigid and breathing in short tight gasps.

"Hannah?"

"Yes?"

"Your brother is still all I ever think about."

"I know. It's okay."

They heard the heavy steps of boots in the snow start up the mound beneath them. They heard the cop slip and slide down. They heard a whispered and deep "Fuck." Heavy steps, kicking into the snow now.

"Hannah?"

"Yes?"

"I think it's admirable they way you keep on with your music."

"Thank you, Laurel."

The cop slipped again. They could hear him breathing heavily below them. Then he turned and walked away. They listened to his steps getting fainter and then they heard the car start and drive away. They poked their heads up and looked below. It was as it had been when they arrived. They looked at each other. "Well, that was interesting," Hannah said.

Laurel nodded. "They call it the hug drug," she said.

The evening before they had driven out to the lake, Laurel and Daphne had gone to see a movie together. Walking home, Daphne had asked Laurel if she had ever thought about having children. "A year ago, I almost decided to, but that's when things with Eliot were getting crazy and it didn't seem like a good idea. I didn't tell anyone at the time, just hung out at my apartment afterwards and took Tylenol Threes. I never told Eliot about it. It seemed sort of academic by that point," Laurel said.

"Oh dear," Daphne said.

"It's okay. I don't think about it as much as I used to. The thing is, it isn't clear to me whether if that had happened earlier on things between us mightn't have turned out differently. Not that I'd ever recommend it as a strategy or anything. But looking back, it seemed like there was a moment there when we needed something to do together. We didn't, so we just started heading away. Old story."

"Does Hannah know about this?" Daphne asked.

"No," Laurel lied, instinctively.

"I won't say anything, of course."

"Thank you."

They walked a little farther. "Why do you ask?"

No answer. They walked on for a few minutes.

"The thing about Greg is that, if pressed, I couldn't actually say that he has ever done or said anything to stop us from getting more serious. What he hasn't done was initiate or *propel* anything. I've chosen to take this as a decision he has made. But these days I'm wondering if that is accurate."

"It is so easy to just concede defeat sometimes," Laurel said.

"Yes. Even if you don't have to."

"Just follow the easy path."

"Well, the familiar one, anyway. Which may not necessarily turn out to be the easier one, after all."

"There are not so many easy ones, actually."

"No."

They walked on. Laurel stopped suddenly, as if to tie her shoe, but she didn't bend down. Daphne didn't notice for a second, and then when she turned to Laurel, her friend started walking again.

"I would help you, either way," Laurel said.

"For how long?" Daphne asked.

"I don't know. As long as I could."

"Which probably isn't eighteen years."

"I know."

"I'm just going to try to not think about it for a few days and then see if it is clearer to me what I should do."

"Good luck."

They walked on.

"I can't believe this is happening to me at my age."

"I know."


The squall scudded across the lake toward them and they could see whitecaps at the edge of the front, and rain driving down obliquely into the lake. The air grew abruptly cold, and the leaves on the poplar trees that lined the beach started to shake. The three women reached into their bags for their sweaters and pulled them on, still sitting. Litter began swirling along the water's edge.

Hannah looked at Daphne. "So what would you do differently?"

"I don't know. *Affiliate* myself somehow."

Laurel: "Have a pickle, dear, we all feel like that at the end of summer."

Hannah rocked forward on her feet and stood. Daphne looked up at her. Laurel held the pickle jar up to her in turn.

"Do you think we're in trouble?" Hannah asked, raising her voice over the wind. "Do you think things probably aren't going to work out for us?" Laurel looked at the sky. The rain was less than a mile away. You could see it hitting the water. Daphne shook her head. Laurel looked at her. "You think?" she asked.

"I'm pretty sure we're going to be okay," Daphne said.

Hannah sat down. She chewed on a pickle. Laurel touched Daphne's arm.

This was in 1998.

After Lukie Oktok shot himself his house was empty for two months. Nobody on the waiting list for a new house would answer their phone during this time. Finally Theresa Kabluitok's mother, who had five of her adult children still living with her as well as four grandchildren, including Theresa's three, picked up the telephone and yelled into it, "Okay, okay, she'll take it."

The place still smelled of Lukie, and even in the carpet you could detect his Stetson cologne. Theresa's ex-husband came around the day she moved in, thinking maybe they would have a chance now that he wouldn't have to take the old woman's abuse in order to live with her. Theresa thought he was not much of a man if his involvement with her and the children was contingent upon elbow room.

The children were delighted by the house. Having room to run and play seemed like an adventure to them. They knew about Lukie's death, of course, and the bad luck he had had, but they were not much put off by the story, were actually pleased to be part of a drama.

The night after she moved in, Theresa sat in the kitchen of her new house and smoked cigarettes and drank tea. Her children were asleep and she thought about luck, how it follows some people and seems to torment others. Lukie had been an unremarkable man before the accident. He was neither good enough nor wicked enough to stand out in anyone's mind. After the accident, the townspeople combed their memories of him, looking for some portent of disaster. With other unfortunates this was almost always successful, but in Lukie's case it was not. He simply had never said enough, done enough, to stick out in anyone's mind. There were not enough details to shape into a revealing anecdote.

Theresa thought that such a state would suit her— to live inconspicuously enough that her end would seem as random and unilluminating to other people as her life, as she lived it, did to her.

# SAW MARKS

This is what is necessary: an axe and a stone; a hundred feet of quarter-inch rope; a parka; one hundred pounds each of flour and rice; ten pounds of baking soda and of salt. Some fishing line and a set net and an ice jig. Twenty or thirty pounds of lard. A grill. A skillet. Some aspirin. A rifle. Really good boots. It is a relief to find a task, even if it is only to make this list. After working in the bush and caring for the man for thirty years, this absence of tasks is unprecedented. Motionlessness feels too much like death, and there has already been enough of that.

In this town of bearded and vinegar-scented men and women, who never bathe or change their socks, you could go crazy, you could light yourself on fire, or wear your underwear on your head, and their drooping eyelids would not flicker. They have the same relationship with one another as do snakes in a winter den. And when the ice in the Churchill River is rotten and ready to go, in early June, there isn't a creature here who doesn't look out at the taiga and long for room enough to eat a meal without being inspected from behind clouds of grey smoke and tightened mouths like cigarette burns in car seats. Gypsy's Pastry Shop and Café on Saturday afternoons: they all think it the Flore. It goes to show you what a sweetened bread roll can come to mean in an empty enough place.

The tree line along the coast of the Hudson Bay hangs a few miles inland and may be seen from the edge of town as a black fringe, sideburns lining the rock face that slopes into the sea. Churchill sits right at the ocean's edge, preferring the eviscerating winds and pack ice to the treed wildness where muskeg monsters thaw and percolate. One conceives of oneself as impotent there—inland, among the trees and bogs—and so one is. It is astonishing to learn how fast a man or woman is, over distance. Except for the wolf, the fastest animal around over distances more than twenty miles. Try this. The first morning in late summer when there is snow on the ground, take the coffeepot off the stove and then go walking. When you pick up a set of deer tracks—you'll know they were made the previous night—start following them at the fastest walk you can sustain. Before nightfall you'll be standing before exhausted slobbering defeat, feeling ashamed. The meat will taste of the day's terror, but the point remains: we are each of us formidable. And it doesn't take a Winnebago to make your way in the world. You'd think we would know this, and speak of it constantly.

Humans are, by disposition and design, lopers. They are pack hunters and seed grubbers who rely on endurance and planning. "Intelligence" is the wrong word for their gift, suggesting as it does their wit and social structure and clever tricks. Anyway, they spent four million years on the Serengeti and they have only been in cities for six or seven thousand years. They are most themselves when they are walking quickly and thinking about the medium term. One has to last, if anything is to make sense.

I find myself thinking about his crinkled eyes and thinning hair: tufts rising preposterously from his ears, like an elf, like Yoda, shaking his gnarled little head. At the end, his own vanity could not stand it and the jokes about his decline had grown steadily more incisive. When he was nearly so weak he could not walk from the bed to the toilet, he had spent a day constructing, out of fishing line and pulleys, an elaborate call bell system, to signal his distress. He laughed the whole time he built it, shaking his head slowly. I was outside for most of that afternoon, splitting wood, and by the time I was done I had a waist-high pile of kindling.

A solidly built eighteen-foot freighter canoe; four paddles, a one-and-a-half-horsepower engine for the upriver work, which means gasoline and oil; a chainsaw; a lamp and fuel, candles, a fish knife and a hunting knife; some books; matches. A lot of matches. You wouldn't want to run out of matches.

The ice leaves all at once most years; the floe edge creeps in through May and spends part of June lingering enticingly close to shore, even though, Jesus Christ, there's a heat wave in Edmonton. Then one day the wind comes from the south and blows hard for a night and a day and then the ice is fractured and dissipating, headed off into the sea in a thousand shards of its previously monolithic self. The moment is spoken of for weeks beforehand and its arrival is predicted as imminent for nearly a month. Living like this, in the anticipation of an event that cannot be influenced or manipulated—living like this changes everything.

And that is about it. Some sutures, maps, of course, and one of those small GPS navigation devices; the miscellaneous category is not so huge—either a thing is imperative and not at all miscellaneous, or else it is too heavy.

The beauty of useful things is worth noticing. Rope, for instance. Run it through your hands: light, pliable— look, you can bend it in half—gorgeous yellow polypropylene rope. A hundred feet of it weighs only a few pounds, but it can hold hundreds of pounds. Thousands, maybe. Incredible. Or maybe more apparent: the canoe. A thousand bucks from the North West Company, solid, lithe, and light—look at it. It weighs seventy pounds itself and can carry half a ton. There is nothing necessarily impersonal about Kevlar—light and strong and warm: functionality is a kind of loveliness. Forest-green and square-sterned, to take the engine, this little shell still paddles easily and could take twice as much gear. The limiting factor is not what it can carry, but what you can. The rope is coiled and laid on the floor beside the canoe. Smooth, mellifluous dark green and canary yellow, at four in the morning these colours sing.

This is not an argument for a strictly utilitarian aesthetic. Ugly things can be useful and useful things ugly—consider rototillers and anuses, for instance—but people who care enough about tools to make and buy good ones want them to be beautiful as well. This is a kind of love. More on that matter later.

The Woods Company of Ottawa has been making packs for fifty years and they do it with love. Simple canvas-and-leather packs, double stitching throughout, reinforced straps and leather anchor points—pure beauty. Three are necessary for this trip, and they are laid in a line beside the rope. The new ones have rubberized nylon lining and internal aluminum frames, but you would never guess it to look at them. They remain as perfectly beautiful as the models of forty years ago. And beside the packs, a down–filled mummy sleeping bag, bright yellow and as warm as baked bread. A Coleman lantern in its carrying case; fuel comes in shiny aluminum bottles. In a snow-covered tent, the lantern is heat as much as it is a light source. One will want to have some fuel around. In case it is necessary, for some reason, to come back before the warm weather returns.

Escape is contained within its own possibilty: even in its planning, a kind of release is already obtained. You line up all the gear here on the floor of the house, going over the list again, trying to think of something light and useful enough to take that has been forgotten. Liberation presents itself even now in the half-light, with the voices from the bar boisterous and raucous drifting in through the window at three in the morning; in the white nights the mania only builds as the ice groans, craving release, and a thousand men and women yearn as well, but the yearnings are more heterogeneous than they seem and nobody really knows what anyone else wants. And, sitting here looking at the gear, on which the winter pay has been spent, there are clearly no more bonds. You could pick up the canoe right now and carry it down to the water, the gear too, and you could be fifty miles upriver by midnight the next day. And you will be, just as soon as the river breaks.

The Northern Store sells magazines. Once there was one called *Survivalist*, which sounded relevant to this undertaking, but all those characters seemed interested in surviving was a gang war. It was less about survival than annihilation. Bazookas and machine guns—idiots. A fish net is the fastest way to get together a quantity of food anyway. Men and guns.

The one for this trip is his single shot .308 and twelve gauge over-under: twenty-two dollars at the Northern Store, twenty years ago. It does not stir me when I hold it; it is heavy and scratched in many places, but it still fits together easily. The rifle shells have a beauty about them, if one likes the shine of brass. There is a power contained in each of the surprisingly heavy metal cylinders. You can hear the gunpowder within when you shake one. It sounds like a salt shaker. You think: this could kill me too.

Good equipment lasts, and you can tell whether it is good the moment you first lift the pack or swing the axe or load the rifle. The parts fit together properly and are neither too loose nor too tight. The difference between a rifle bolt that is work to operate and one that is not is impossible to appreciate until a well-made rifle is held. And once that has happened there is no going back. Why would someone bother with a cheap knife that won't hold an edge if they knew that good ones do?

I remember when I was teaching in Winnipeg and he was trying to persuade me to come up here and live with him. Once, there was an empty seat on a government plane coming down and he caught it. I met him at an all-night café on McDermott Avenue at three in the morning and we walked to Oman Creek Park and sat on a bench and kissed quietly by the river. It was early April and we were both very cold. We sat there kissing with our teeth chattering. And then the flight was returning and I went to the airport with him and saw him off. I remember this. It was 1976. A Thursday.

This house was made with good equipment, and the sawn spruce and cedar bear cut marks that are twenty years old. It is clear that the timbers were measured carefully and there are no cracks anywhere. Things fit together, each log lies true on the other, and the saws and planes and drill bits, long discarded, have left their importance here. Their meaning was realized as the edges wore down, were sharpened, and wore down again. Eventually the tools were worn out and he threw them away, but by then they had turned themselves into the beauty of right angles and straight edges. And these doorjambs and windowsills and rafters make it matter that the tools were made well. The saw marks say so.

When my sister heard that he was finally gone, she sent her daughter up to see me. I picked her up at the train station, and in the truck I told her that I had retired and would not teach in the fall. She asked me why, and I told her that I was tired. I took her for lunch at Gypsy's and she asked me how I was doing. I kept saying fine and she kept coming back to the question. Clearly her mother was alarmed. I told her to tell her mother not to worry and that I was planning on going travelling for the rest of the summer and the winter. She looked surprised at this and said that she thought that was a good idea, going travelling. Either with another woman, or, searching my eyes, alone? That's still good, she said. Then she asked me where I was going. I said I wasn't exactly sure, yet. She said there was lots of time to look at the schedules, watch for seat sales.

And then we drove back to my house, and I let her in, and she stopped in the doorway looking at all the gear lined up so neatly in the living room. She asked me how long I was going into the bush for. I told you, I said. She replied that the loneliness goes away eventually. I told her that that was nothing to wish for. She'd been divorced twice and she just blinked at me.

This was in 1997.

When Cora heard of the old woman's disappearance she recalled that her mother had spoken of this woman, who had quit her job years ago to go north, following a man to Churchill. Cora's mother had taught with her in the city for three years and they had eaten lunch together, every day in the library, unless one of them was on playground duty. Her departure was abrupt. Cora's mother had found a letter in her mailbox one morning that said: "My advice would be to not marry him. His ambivalence will not resolve."

And it did not. But, Cora thought, over time it had settled into something less agitating. Her parents were now at ease with one another, and somehow pleased, as if neither had expected things to turn out as well as they had.

Cora and her friends seemed incapable of this kind of patience. As details of the disappeared woman's life filtered out, through the gossip of her acquaintances to Cora's mother, and then to Cora, broad similarities between her life and Cora's were apparent. Cora lived in a small, cold place, just as the old woman had. But loneliness was, for Cora, like the snow—contained within the idea of the place itself. It was not something she thought could be effectively resisted. The idea of the old woman punctured Cora a little; the old woman's success in building a redoubt of companionship and faith, surrounded by all that tundra, cast Cora's acquiescence in a different light. She felt cynical and less brave.

She thought about this as she drank whisky and listened to the wind. There was not an obvious solution.

# BOATBUILDING

With a good enough book you can do anything. You could rebuild a carburetor, walk across a desert, learn Mandarin, become proficient in needlepoint. None of us is the first to be baffled by compound curves or aphid infestation. Our salvation lies in the scalp scratching of our predecessors, and this is how the world improves.

*Boatbuilding*, by Howard I. Chapelle, has instructed three generations of shipwrights in the building of wooden boats. It was first published in 1941, and its clear and patient prose has calmed the panicked faces of inexperienced builders of wooden boats ever since. Chapelle makes the reader breathe slowly, and think more clearly, as the intricacy of sheer lines and rabbet joints are contemplated. Building a wooden boat is an act of daunting complexity, and Mr. Chapelle's book takes the neophyte by the hand and approaches the task one step at a time, soothing and encouraging. It's as good as a cup of Ovaltine.

The first chapter is devoted to lofting. According to Mr. Chapelle, the care taken with the lofting of a boat is more important than any given act involving wood. The first step of lofting is the drawing of a full-scale plan of the boat's hull on a suitable floor. Concentric hull lines taper together sinuously over the floor the boat is to be built upon. Using these lines as a guide, one cuts out full-size cardboard outlines of the important beams that will subsequently form the curves of the hull.

Churchill served Carol's purposes well. It was on the northern sea and it was a long way away from anyone who knew her. When she arrived on the train, fresh from her appalling family, she had never known anyone who had built a boat, and so she began her own effort with a number of misconceptions and romantic but distorted images of the task. She imagined herself with a plane, bent over an oaken beam, pausing frequently to brush aromatic shavings from her forehead in an indefatigable-and-pant-suited Katharine Hepburn sort of way. She couldn't but feel disappointed when she realized how much time she would have to spend before sawing into the first plank.

The autumnal equinox saw her in her kitchen, by lamplight, cutting out hundreds of cardboard posts, planks, ribbands, and rabbets. Her closets grew wild with jutting bits of curved cardboard, numbered and cross-indexed against the plans. Every night she would sweep out the leavings of that day's session, and not since high school had she held her tongue between her teeth as she guided scissors down pencil-scribed cardboard, concentrating like a jeweller.

As the bits of her cardboard proto-boat accumulated, she steadily developed more respect for the immensity of her undertaking. She was surprised, for instance, to learn how many pieces there would be in the keel that she would lay. This was naive; a single block of wood would be prone to splitting and twist. She understood that. Still, she thought, if there were to be a part of the vessel that would be whole and of a piece, you'd think it would be the keel, stabilizing everything through its own ponderous weight. The idea appealed to her—she liked the suggestion of constancy and submerged strength. (Attributes found even less in her own life these days than previously; soon she'd have to build a trough beside her bed's headboard to spare the pillowcases.)

But the solitary load bearer works better in Homeric epics and popular films than in a working boat. As a matter of engineering principle, better by far to distribute the strain as much as possible; overlap and overlie at every opportunity. Single members fail—even if they're sturdy enough at the outset, there's no avoiding deep faults, hidden rot. Shared loads preserve the whole. Any failure analysis demonstrates it: singularity is poor design. In the evening, in front of the radio in the kitchen trying to find music somewhere, this is as evident as a collapsed bridge.

Mr. Chapelle reminds us: design is compromise.

In Etobicoke, where Carol lived for twenty years, and where her husband remained and where her sixteen-year-old daughter, presumably, also remained, it was still summer, practically. Brandy would be wearing halter tops with sequins and small animals embroidered over her breasts. There would be dark circles under her eyes and her right index finger would be orange from the Player's Plain habit she had acquired. There would be either the suggestion of or a frank and unreserved sneer on her lips, depending on her mood.

She would be sitting on the sidewalk beside the 7-Eleven in her Toronto suburb and reading whatever magazine she had just shoplifted. Parents of Brandy's friends had told Carol that she was okay, was couch-surfing for now. But with her gone, the house had been unbearable. Carol hadn't anticipated this but neither had it entirely surprised her. The immediate agony of Brandy had distracted her from the less insistent but all-encompassing and even less bearable dread of the rest of Carol's life. And it wasn't like her daughter's return was going to be a relief. At least for more than thirty seconds.

Jim would be playing Myst on his computer, which is what he had been doing for most of the last four years. The seasons mattered less to him. He had long since grown fat and white as Oreo cookie filling in that basement, emerging long enough to eat and fall asleep on the couch and go to work in the morning, where nobody at Robinson's Plumbing Supply seemed to think there was anything wrong with him. Although, clearly, that Carol had some "anger issues," they would say at Christmas parties, nodding sympathetically in his direction. The fuckers.

The workshed, which she had rented together with the cabin beside it, still smelled of muskrat pelts and motor oil. But the shed's concrete floor would be just large enough to fit the hull, and its doors would permit the unrigged boat to exit too. That, and the presence of the sea a half mile from the house, made renting the place inevitable. The owner was a civil servant named Harry Postelwaithe who had lived and worked in Churchill for twenty vaguely hostile and eccentric years, administering the harbour for the federal government. He had slipped a disc and could no longer contemplate a winter out here at Goose Creek, seven miles from town, with no electricity or running water, and all that snow shovelling and wood splitting. He had taken one of the government apartments in town so he could shuffle across the street to work during this, his final winter, before retiring to the Okanagan Valley. Postelwaithe remembered the Okanagan from his youth as unspoiled orchards from north to south and seemed to believe it had remained ever so. In her few pause-laden conversations with him, Carol had not disabused him of his idea of persistent paradise in the interior of British Columbia.

Living in town suited Postelwaithe poorly. He drove out to his old house in his pickup truck almost daily at first and then less often as the winter progressed, making sure everything was okay, the roof hadn't started leaking with the autumn rains, the beavers hadn't dammed up the creek in the back again. She found him, once, in the shed at night, looking at her piles of timber and sawdust, cedar planking and the paper forms all around. They looked at one another, startled—each of them too embarrassed to ask, or explain.

The neighbours had not come visiting. There, thankfully, had been no casseroles. She had had far more privacy than she had expected. It was not clear to her how pleased she should be about this. Exile is like that. It's tough to know how much you want to succeed.

The city had not forgotten her. Every few weeks a letter arrived, or a message was left on her answering machine. She had not replied to any of them yet, but she intended to. She imagined her friends would give her some grace, though she'd been gone half a year already. Babies would have been born, people would have died. Rumination along these lines was abruptly halted and redirected to the matter at hand. Carvel planking versus lapstrake;

sloop or ketch; cutter head or not; there were many decisions, and this was as she had planned. All in all, her strategy had been effective. She went weeks without thinking about the world beyond her little homestead.

When she arrived it had been late winter and now it was almost winter again. She had spent part of the summer laying in stores for the winter. Postelwaithe had built a greenhouse, and in it a garden had risen and sagged; the squashes lay split and rotten upon one another, the potatoes still waited to be dug. The tomatoes had long since expired.

Her cold cellar was filled with blueberry and Saskatoon jam and apple butter and stewed tomatoes and turnips and beets and sweet potatoes. In the freezer lay a dozen dressed and plucked chickens, a couple of geese, some ducks, and half a lamb. Smoked hams hung from the rafter, a wheel of cheese was covered with cloth, and there were bottles of wine and cider. Beside the house were three cords of birch; the fireplace and the stove chimneys had been scrubbed down to bare brick. Bookshelves filled her bedroom. The library she had brought up here contained many graduate degrees' worth of reading on astronomy and marine biology and, of course, boatwrighting and timber curing and celestial navigation.

The food and the books and the cordwood inspired in her a feeling of legitimacy or wherewithal that allowed her to imagine herself equal to this business.

This reasoning was dubious, she would concede. The possession of food, fuel, and information composed only a small part of what was necessary to build a boat, but that feeling—of capability, resourcefulness, intactness—was indispensable. Indeed, the whole object of this enterprise.

By early October she had finished the lofting of the individual pieces and she was ready to begin laying out the lines of the boat. This is normally done with chalk, on the work floor, she read. The sheer lines describe the curve the hull makes as it arches from the stern around to the stem, and was a complicated thing to translate from tenth-scale plans to her motor-oil-stained concrete. She studied the drawings for days, drinking coffee with Irish whiskey, in the barn. Houses are built sensibly, with right angles and vertical lines, ninety degrees being "right" and vertical being "true." The language is dominated by house builders, as opposed to boatbuilders.

A static structure bears perpendicular surfaces well. The column reliably supports loads only when vertical and straight; when gravity is the sole antagonist, flat continuous planes at right angles to one another make compelling sense. The moment the construction is put into motion, all this changes. Sleek and graceful curves are as much a demand of fluid dynamics as they are of aesthetics, or more. The thin-hipped curves of the Spitfire would have been sacrificed in an instant for economy of construction had they not been the reason it was so fast. In the complicated mathematics of fluid dynamics the intuitive sense of what looks best—that is, most graceful and supple—was for many years the most reliable design criterion for ships and aircraft. Before computers, the argument for an aesthetic sensibility in the design of vessels was an easy one. It is gratifying that in these instances beauty proved correct, if not right, in the perpendicular sense.

She had just finished stapling the last cardboard bulwark together, and was returning to the kitchen for more whiskey, when she saw the snow on the ground. It was late afternoon and it must have been snowing for most of the day—already it was a foot deep. She stopped abruptly and stared at the sky, alarmed that it was winter already and she had not yet affixed even a single bit of wood to another. She returned to the barn to look at her cardboard skeleton vessel, numbered and inscribed. It seemed improbable and pathetic. Too light, too much like a high school art project to have any real credibility. This, after months of work.

She stalked back across the yard and into her kitchen, turning on the lights as she entered. The yard light was surrounded by a cone of wet silver snow, like vaporized mercury. She looked at the scarred maple table that dominated the room, covered with boat plans and empty rolls of tape. She bit her cheek to stop the panic welling up in her, and walked quickly into the living room. Through a window she could see the sky thickening with snow. She closed her eyes. She could be crazy, she thought. She picked up the telephone. When Jim answered she hung up. She wondered for a moment if he had gotten caller display since she had left. Probably not. Would he even know about star sixty-nine? Probably not. She wondered about Brandy and then forced herself to stop.

Back to the barn. Hours after midnight, and drunk. Cardboard or no, it had a certain grace about it. From here on in, timber would replace cardboard in a successions of transplantations like wax for bronze. She had made a thing. It wasn't nothing.

When Brandy was born she had black hair as thick as a kewpie doll's, and was more beautiful than can be said. Eyes like little wrinkles in a morel, her wee belly as flat as a cut cheese, her sex another folded cloth, feet little nubbins of bone and skin, each like a baby rodent. Even distractible Jim's attention was caught for a few months, and they huddled together in that awful house-just-like-the-one-beside-it-except-that-theirs-was-the-mirror-image and just grinned, all three of them, for six months.

The day after her plans arrived in the mail she had driven into town and placed her lumber order at the Northern Store. For the planking she would use yellow cedar, and for the ribs and frames white oak. It was astonishingly expensive to buy such wood clear of knots and defects. When she wrote out the cheque the clerk had scrutinized the distant city's address on it and her signature. He'd have to wait to place the order until it cleared the bank, it's policy. She nodded.

She climbed to the loft of the shed, where the lumber was stored, and removed the tarps. The cedar's fragrance leaped up to her, like too much scent, and she could barely wait to cut into it and breathe in the perfumed air. The oak was rough and needed planing, but beneath the saw marks the hard open grain looked out at her. She held a length to her cheek and licked it. It tasted bitter, like dried carrot greens.

In laying the ballast keel and joining it to the backbone, it must be ensured that the whole member lies plumb and true, along all three axes. Along the horizontal axis the ribs must rise vertically in every instance; no cant forward or aft can be allowed if the subsequent joinery work of deck and planking is to proceed. And it would never do to have the keel cocked, however subtly, off to port or starboard—such a vessel would never hold a reliable course; nor can it be rotated even minutely around its longitudinal axis—the resulting displacement of the ballast would put the centre of gravity well outboard and the vessel would list drunkenly the moment she was launched, circling always in the direction of her list, as if on tether to some hidden, submarine anchor.

She had bought good tools, at Mr. Chapelle's instruction, and had them shipped up on the rail line a few weeks after she arrived. Her thickness planer was worth as much as a small car, her band and table saws almost as much again. Along one wall of the shed she had built a workbench out of clean, sanded white pine, and the pegboard above it held her Swedish chisels and mallets and handsaws. As they had arrived in cases she had taken them out and examined each one like it was artwork, and oiled and rubbed them until the act was feeling disconcertingly sexual. The workbench was the first thing she ever made out of wood. It had taken her three starts and nearly a week. But in the end it was solid and stable, and in building it, she was persuaded that she really could build a boat, which made the bench a success twice over. And the cheques drawn on their bank account had kept clearing. He must have cashed in some of their mutual funds.

Making the mould in which to cast the lead ballast keel was the first really difficult thing she had to do. In the course of all the lofting work, she had cut out a series of ovoid patterns—cross sections—which laid out the lines of the ballast keel, growing larger from bottom to top. From these she sawed corresponding blocks out of two-inch white pine planks. Stacked on top of one another and bolted together, they composed the mould form. As she assembled the form, the curves of the hull came to be hinted at in the alignment of these blocks. The stepwise progression of the forms still had to be faired out, made flush.

An adze looks like a curved chisel attached at right angles to an axe handle—an ice pick but with a blade. It is a fierce-looking device and, Mr. Chapelle warned her, causes more injury in the shipyard than practically any other tool. Picturing his lined, concerned face, she swung it slowly and carefully. Standing over the wooden mould, swinging the blade between her legs like a croquet mallet, she thought, This could get dangerous. And then she set the adze down and lit another lamp, to better light the workshop. She resumed her chipping. You get hurried or frightened doing this sort of work and you lose a leg.

By the time Brandy started grade five, still a baby, her mother thought, things were already going badly. Each morning she drove Brandy to school, and when she got back Jim would have left for work. At nine forty-five she got into the car and drove to the library where she worked. When she got home in the afternoon, Brandy and Jim would already be there, each going about his or her business. For the next few years, Brandy played with the neighbourhood girls after school: hours and hours up in her bedroom giggling. At some point one of them—over the years they had all had a turn, all except Brandy—would emerge crying. That's what they did, each and every day. And whenever there were variations—holidays, weekends, extended tantrums—everyone involved prayed for the routine to resume.

~

To melt the lead enough to get it to flow into the mould, she needed a casting pot, a container to hold the molten metal. The book suggested she use an old cast-iron bathtub. She had driven to the town dump, a little skeptically, and she had brought an old, chipped, claw-footed lovely back to her yard. She placed wooden blocks under each of the paws and lit a coal fire beneath the tub. She ran a steel pipe from the bath drain to the casting mould. This all struck her as a preposterous way to cast metal.

It took her days to get the tub hot enough to melt her lead blocks. In the end she had to buy a half-dozen thirty-pound propane tanks from the Northern Store, with torch heads that she set to fire all along the bottom of the tub. She had set this all up outside in the yard, concerned about fire in the workshed, but the wind seemed to dispel every bit of heat she generated the instant it was created, and these were long, cold days.

When the lead was finally hot enough—and it had to be much hotter than simply the melting point, or it would just solidify in the drain—she opened the valve and watched the lead drain slowly out of the tub. It ran nicely onto the mould, settling over it like thick silver syrup, smoking against the wooden form and glistening and steaming in the cold air. Every snowflake that landed on it hissed. The propane torches roared.

The ribs of the boat came next. Once again, she studied the loftwork she had prepared and was moved by the fluid beauty of the complex curves she'd described. She had assumed that the ribs could be cut all of a piece out of larger blocks, and she was surprised to learn that even if timber of sufficient size had been available to allow that, the grain had to follow the curves of the ribs or else the member was irredeemably weakened. The wood wasn't statuary—it couldn't be chipped into the desired shape as if it had no grain, as if it possessed no intrinsic character.

To pressure-steam wood, you need a container that seals tightly. The manufacture of a welded steel box that would serve as the pressure cooker daunted her a little. She would have to learn to weld. And the consequences of a shabbily made steam box struck her as perilous.

There was a great deal of discussion from Chapelle about the need for a sufficient number of hands to handle the steamed wood, to get it bent onto the frame before it cooled. She considered this advice and concluded that she would have to make up with preparation for what she lacked in manpower. She cleared out half the floor space in the shed for this part of the operation. Another trip into town to buy an arc welder and steel plate and hinges and sealing rubber. And a welding-for-beginners manual.

She had told herself that her daughter hadn't become a bad kid—how could there be a bad kid?—that she was just acting out, that if she could just get Jim to pay a little more attention to her, if she could just get this family back on track together, then it would be clear that she was a lovely little girl, just as she always had been.

She had believed, despite the available evidence, that it was impossible to screw up, impossible to make anything other than an innately sweet and ultimately lovely daughter, that no effort was required beyond that of endurance, as if the outcome was preordained. You could just slip into stupor and sleepwalk through her life as you sleepwalked through your own, and nothing bad would come of it and certainly there was no responsibility to be taken for anything bad that did. She sat on the step of the shed, remembering this; the air inside was still settling and sawdust was precipitating out onto every horizontal surface and she hit herself in the centre of her forehead steadily, as if she were driving in a stubborn dowel.

When the wedding-present silverware disappeared and Brandy proposed that a burglar had got it in the middle of the night, but had taken nothing else, Carol had seized her and pulled her close, both of them shaking. They held one another for maybe an hour, long after Jim had gone back down to the basement, and then they released each other and never referred to the matter again.

These days, on the Arctic coast, passed for Carol without any real sense of time. A day was as long as what she managed to get done. Some days didn't exist at all, as when she mismeasured a piece of wood and was left at the end of the day where she had started. Some days stretched on and on, and task after task was completed, and she felt like she could do anything, charging from one perfect fit to another, glue curing flawlessly, joints so tight you'd think the pieces only lately split from one another by an especially sharp and slim blade. Days like that were unusual, but occurred often enough to keep her going.

She awoke in the mornings to an alarmingly cold house; she couldn't seem to find a way to keep the stove stoked. Most nights she fell asleep in the living room listening to late-night radio, then woke at some point and ran shrieking through her abruptly frozen house into her stiff-from-the-temperature bedsheets. In the morning the house seemed like it could not be any warmer than the air outside, the sheets around her face soggy from condensation.

And then, lighting the stove, heating the water for a bath and her oatmeal and coffee. She took extravagant care over the preparation of oatmeal, which she came to appreciate as she never had in the course of her life in the city. She boiled it, lavishly, in apple cider with nutmeg and cinnamon sticks and vanilla beans. Breakfast was hard to learn to eat alone, and by making a big enough production of it she found that she could divert her attention almost completely from her isolation.

In the Northern Store they had looked at her dubiously when she said that she wanted something with which she could weld eighth-inch steel plate, but didn't know what exactly, did they have any advice for her? The older man who had been working when she ordered her lumber and the lead and the rest of the supplies she had needed hadn't been present but rather a younger man, his son presumably. The son had the younger man's need to elevate himself, and he lifted his eyebrows archly and inquired whether she would be interested in an inert gas machine, or a simple arc welder, or was she thinking oxyacetylene, or what. Asshole. She had asked him what colour each came in.

On the way out of town she stopped at Gypsy's Café and Bakery for a glass of beer and a pork chop. Postelwaithe was there, eating by himself. When she saw him she lifted up her plate and glass and walked up to his table and asked if she could join him. He looked surprised, but assented.

"How is your boat coming along?" he asked, raising his bushy eyebrows. She had never mentioned it to another person and until this moment it had felt like it existed only within her.

"Fine," she said, tucking into her pork chop.

"What are you going to do with the boat when you are done?" he asked

"Launch it," she said, chewing.

He nodded. "Here?"

"It's the reason I came here," she said. "The ocean being so close."

"Good a reason as any," he said.

"Better than most," she said, enjoying the ranch-hand cadence to their speech.

"You said a mouthful there," he said. She swallowed her chop and nodded.


Welding isn't as hard as it looks. The noise and that bright light are frightening at first but you won't get hurt if you keep your glasses on and for God's sake don't go picking up anything before you've doused it, even if it's been many minutes since you heated it and the flange looks like it's room-temperature. You really do need proper leather welding gloves (and a new pair after manoeuvres like that) and coveralls that can't trap sparks. Keep the rod moving: too fast and the bead will be thin and inter-rupted, too slowly and you'll melt through the plate, leaving holes in the seam. It takes a day or two to start to get the hang of it. And then you'll get an idea of just how much there is to know. Steel is supposed to be a snap compared to aluminum or titanium. Even stainless steel is a lot tougher than plain steel. She found herself bent under the steel tube chairs in her kitchen, studying the neat little beads that she had never noticed before.

The steam box was, in the end, simply a large coffin-shaped box made out of excessively welded steel plate. In it were racks upon which she could lay precut pieces of wood, and on the bottom of the box was a large pan that held water. Protruding out of the top, through fittings that had been rewelded many times, were a metal thermometer and a pressure gauge.

The first time she fired it up was an experiment. She inserted a piece of oak, filled the water tank, and sealed the box. Then she lit the fire beneath it. Within twenty minutes the pressure and temperature had reached the prescribed levels. She waited another three hours and then she released the steam out of the valve. When she opened the box she could hardly breathe for the clouds enveloping her. All she could smell was the scent of oak steamed to three hundred degrees and as pungent as a poached fish. She took the piece out with long tongs and quickly manoeuvred the limp board onto the clamp table. There she tightened and adjusted the clamps until the beam described the smooth arc of the hull's cross section, like one half of a wineglass, cut lengthwise.

When the wood had cooled, she loosened off the clamps and examined the beam. It retained the graceful curve she had impressed upon it. She sat on a sawhorse, admiring it. This had been a straight and solid oak beam. You could have carved it. Now, cold, its new bend would hardly bend itself when she put all her weight on it. This was the best thing she had done so far.

When that poor girl's mother had called to tell her what Brandy had done to her daughter, Carol had been unable to say even a word in reply. She listened to the other woman's anger abstractly, like she was listening in on one of those times that the telephone circuits get crossed and strangers start talking back and forth, unaware of their listener. It was only when she paused after the long bitter monologue and accusation that Carol snapped to, and expressed regret and sympathy for the clothes, the bruising, and the ripped earlobe, from where the girl's earring had been caught. She offered to pay for the clothes. The other woman was baffled by the proposal.

With the ribs of the boat lined up protruding and parallel out of the keel, the boat looked more than ever like the skeletal fish it was in her imagination, belly to the sky, or, in this instance, the ceiling of the increasingly crowded shop. It felt to her now that she was making real progress. She started the planking, with the fragrant yellow cedar, an hour after the last rib was in place. She could see the vessel forming itself rapidly now, her eyes closed, sitting on a sawhorse and drinking whiskey, and she pictured the bow surging into the sea

By March the days were getting longer again and the planking and decking were complete. Carol had opted for a very spare interior. Her berth was narrow and enclosed. The galley consisted only of a two-burner kerosene stove and some counter space and a sink. There was no refrigerator, no pressurized water, only a bronze hand pump. There were kerosene lamps, ordered from a chandlery in Vancouver, which swung from the cabin top. When she lit them, the whole boat glowed orange, like very oblique sunlight in late autumn. On relatively warm nights, she took to sleeping in the boat, on her berth. In the shed, among the sawdust and shavings, she imagined she could hear the sea breaking around her and that she was a thousand miles into it.

She had ordered a wooden mast that had been shipped up on the train, arousing the curiosity of everyone at the train station, the day she had driven into town to pick it up. As she had driven it home, the mast jutting out fifteen feet ahead of and behind her pickup, everyone who saw her stepped outside onto the side of the road to stare.

The chandlery had also sent up ready-made stainless-steel stays and sails and a hundred-fathom roll of half-inch Dacron line, for the running rigging. These had arrived in great bundles that she dragged to her truck box, without explanation or discussion, and unloaded into her shed with a growing sense of delight.

In June she called Postelwaithe and asked him to help her launch her boat. He was in the process of putting his things on the train, he said. Do you have time to give me a hand, she asked. I suppose I do, he said.

The next weekend they pulled the boat into town, mounted on a sledge Carol had built. The pulling was done with a Caterpillar tractor Postelwaithe had borrowed from the harbour. The boat appeared in town at noon that Saturday, and by the time they made it down to the harbour, where Postelwaithe had arranged for a crane, they had acquired an entourage of curious onlookers. Postelwaithe asked Carol what she was naming her boat. She said she hadn't decided yet. He nodded, and climbed into the crane cab. Carol's boat was set in the water and it floated serenely. The next day Postelwaithe's replacement was flying in. Postelwaithe would fly out a week later. He said he was going to be busy that week. Carol nodded. She thanked him for his help. He said you're welcome. He asked if she would be staying on in the house. She said she supposed not. He said he thought he would try to sell the place to the man replacing him. Carol asked if the man would be interested in buying a table saw. Postelwaithe said he'd be happy to ask.

On the boat that night, bobbing against the wharf beside the grain elevators, Carol stared out at the mouth of the Churchill River and beyond, at the sea. She had made a very fine boat. It was something.

When she first left Etobicoke, she had stayed in the True North Motel in Sault Ste. Marie. Drinking whiskey by noon most days, and smoking cigarettes in a steady succession, lighting one off the other, and filling up aluminum Coke cans until little mounds of ash trickled down them. Those days were the worst thing she had ever known. A man was staying in the room next to hers and watched pornography all afternoon and then went out someplace until three in the morning. It felt to her like her life had been ruined, that she had ruined her life. It was the first time she ever conceived that as possible, and not as melodramatic overstatement.

In late June, the twilight in Churchill lasts until shortly before dawn, and at one in the morning she came up top, to urinate. The sky stretched out before her in a glorious arc of orange and pink. Beneath her, and above her, was beauty that was unlike anything she had known. She looked at it through her binoculars, and the colour was even more vivid and the sky even brighter. She moved her feet and felt the dry, tight teak planking creak slightly. Her little boat was in the water and floating. There had been no leaks; she had checked the bilge every twenty minutes for hours after the launch. Dawn would emerge out of dusk in another hour or two.

The Churchill River was nearly a mile wide here at its mouth, and it looked like a broad, cold lake. Beluga whales had been surfacing in it all evening, but at this moment she could no longer hear them. Beyond the bar, the Hudson Bay stretched to the horizon, littered with fractured pans of ice.

The open water in the river merged into Hudson Bay, which flowed in turn past Baffin Island and through

Davis Strait to the Labrador Coast, the North Atlantic, and from there to the world. The water went everywhere. Even home, if she wanted.

This was in 1999.

Every time the woman on the other side of the wall gasped, he could hear the saliva snapping as her mouth opened. His bed swayed in sympathy to theirs and neither of the senses unavailable to him, visual and olfactory, was difficult to summon up on his own.

Jim thought, if he could just have this, it would be enough of a simulation of desire for his purposes.

And then he thought: How ridiculous I am. And he opened the minibar and then looked out on the level landscape of low buildings and glowing summer-night horizons extending away from him, and he wondered why he imagined his life might be different, given what he knew of himself.

# THE PERSEID SHOWER

"Will you look at this," my father asks, with the wonderment of unexpected good fortune. "Now who would just throw this out?"

He is holding a rubber sealing ring the size of a hula hoop from an old washing machine, inspecting it carefully, running his thumbnails through the grooves looking for cracks. Not even a blemish. He is wearing a green cotton work shirt and trousers. We are at the Dunsmuir municipal garbage dump. I am sitting in the truck cab. He is exploring.

"Dad," I say.

"No, Bob, really," he says. And he takes out his tape measure, trying to judge the diameter. "Last week I paid thirty-four dollars for a new one just like it." I lean my head against the truck window and slide down in the seat. The Hutterites poking through a pile farther down look up at his excitement and begin sidling toward him, curious but polite. I shut my eyes. I am appalled. I am fourteen years old. He looks over at me; he sees my disapproval. And he sets the sealing ring down on the pile.

"Pretty good one over here!" he calls to the bearded old men and babushka-clad women, all polka-dotted kerchiefs and coarse woollen trousers. Their children sit in their trucks, slouching and likewise appalled, albeit less vocal. An old man comes closer and my father picks up the ring again and hands it to him. The old man smiles thank you. My father grins back, delighted that the sealing ring is saved. He ambles along the line of smoking detritus, talking to himself. I turn on the radio. The new John Lennon song buzzes through lost change and abandoned bubble gum. It is Sunday afternoon and I have just started smoking cigarettes. My twin brother, Albert, has already retreated into a cavern of science-fiction books and fierce resolution. We hardly see him, except on his way to Star Trek conventions in the city. That whole summer he was at physics camp and none of us had any idea what went on there.

We incinerated our own garbage in forty-gallon oil drums in the backyard. The drums burned through quickly and once a month we had to drive to the dump to empty the ashes and scout for a better barrel. The best were the dented but practically new oil drums the Esso bulk dealer dropped off on Friday afternoons. These went quickly, but others, trading up, left in exchange barrels with considerable life left in them yet, and Dad was happy to take these, as well. Few would ever consider using *our* rejects—in the bio-niche of the Dunsmuir garbage dump, we were bottom feeders. For my father at least, this was a point of pride.

For as long as I can remember it has been the same with him: Saturday and Sunday afternoons he is in the garden, or the basement, one minute and the next he is suddenly absent. You look through the garage, the tool-shed, but no answer. Then the truck rumbles up the driveway and from the kitchen window he can be observed furtively carrying boxes into the garage, there to sort and contemplate.

I remember one time I went out there and found him dismantling old radios and humming. We sat there most of the afternoon, me just watching him putter, try-ing to discern an endpoint, or goal, of all this. In another three or four months the radios would be thrown out again, under the insistent gaze of my mother, but he didn't care. For now, he was immersed in his booty, and anyway, who knew what fresh treasure would lie within the next box? Not me.

"Isn't this great stuff? These things must be forty years old. Look, this radio here looks like it was taken care of. I wonder if I can get it to work."

"Dad, where on earth do you think you would get new parts for these things?" I say, shaking my head. He looks up at my tone. He blinks.

"From each other maybe."

"They're mostly not even the same make, Dad."

"They didn't make things as complicated in those days, they might work even so. Hand me that Phillips screwdriver behind you? No, the little one, thanks."

The next week it would be vacuum cleaners, the following one, bicycles. The things that went in there astonish me even in recollection—where did he find a Depression-era Hebrew typewriter with a seized roller? (In the ditch, he said.)

The other thing we did on the weekends was go to model airplane shows. My father built himself a radio-controlled miniature P-51 Mustang fighter that he used to fly for hours out behind the house. He built it from a kit and every time he ran into snags in the course of building it, he would go to one of the model airplane shows in the vicinity and ask people what he should do. Looking back at it, I don't know why we didn't just join one of the clubs. Shyness, I suppose. In the meantime, he and I got to know the secondary road network of southern Manitoba intimately, through our weekend journeys to small-town airports and abandoned Second World War landing strips, looking for the Neepawa Fly-O-Rama, the Teulon Tailspin.

I remember walking with him up and down the rows and rows of model airplanes, all hovered over by fat men in plaid sport shirts and sunglasses. My dad liked the racers, sleek and polished and unadorned. I liked the military models, some of which carried real (well, real-looking) little bombs that had caps in them that would explode with a bang when dropped. At these shows they sometimes had precision bombing contests, with little bridges and miniature factories built out of balsa wood. I was constantly disappointed that the little bangs and puffs of smoke always left the balsa-wood structures largely intact.

In the evenings there would be seminars on new construction techniques, and there would be displays set up by the hobby supply salesmen who hung out at these shows and could smell my father approaching, like he was a bruised and bleeding tuna fish, and they Ravenous Killer Sharks of the Deep.

One night we were sitting in a big canvas tent; it was mid-summer and the flies and moths flickered around the fastidiously hung Chinese lanterns like biological dust demons. There was a speaker, at the front, talking about the essentials of laminated-fibreglass wing construction. My father was on the edge of his seat, scribbling down notes in his little brown notebook with his mechanical pencil—this was exactly what he needed. I knew because we had spent most evenings of the previous month up late in the garage, trying to get the resin thin enough to meet the weight specifications, yet still thick enough to bind properly to the belts of fibreglass. Even I was a little excited at the prospect of finding out what we had been doing wrong.

"But that's pretty much all the time I have to talk about the principles of building with fibreglass. However I do have a few minutes to talk about this new formed-polystyrene process you've all been hearing about." Everyone in the room stirred and leaned forward. For everyone but us neophytes the earlier talk had been pretty old hat. My father and I looked at each other.

"Ask him," I said.

"He didn't talk about making the resin at all, did he?" my father said, flipping through his notes.

"No—ask him now, before he gets going again." And my father looked up.

"*Ask* him," I hissed.

"Slide please," the model airplane expert said, and the lights fell. The crowd breathed in as one at the sight of the wing cross section before them. "I thought you'd like this part," the man said.

When the speaker had concluded his musings on formed polystyrene my father and I joined the scrum around the podium, each of us hungry for the model airplane expert's wisdom on matters ranging from retractable landing gears to the future of aeronautical modelling itself. Each time an opening in the conversation seemed to be appearing a hobbyist named Walt or Stan or Herb would crowd in with a question about any aspect of the modelling world except resin preparation. My father kept raising his finger haltingly and smiling as Walt or Herb or Stan pushed forward with their more sophisticated problems. Then, without warning, the expert looked at his watch, said something about having to make Saskatoon the following afternoon, mumbled goodbyes, and sprinted off to the parking lot huffing and puffing. We watched his car drive away. All the way home I didn't say a word.

The summer I turned sixteen, my mother, my father, and I all agreed that I should get work, for the usual generationally disparate reasons: maturity, work ethic, learning the value of a dollar—this against pizza, gasoline, and buying my own personal care items and intoxicants. My mother could not have remained uninvolved in such an undertaking, and so when she came home one day with the news that she had been speaking to the owner of the adult video store, Blue Moon Videos, which was in the same strip mall as my father's dental practice, and that the owner thought he needed some help, I accepted her contribution as inevitable. *Now you just go down there tomorrow afternoon, he's looking forward to meeting you, don't be so shy all the time.*

The owner's name was Bobby Sigrun and he had taken a drubbing in the housecrafts business for ten years before he had had a moment of truth one morning in the late seventies and saw the direction of the future in small-volume retailing: goodbye macramé, hello Long Dong Silver. He laughed easily and hired me in minutes. Before I knew it I was the general labourer/driver/shop clerk of the Municipality of Dunsmuir's cultural and moral low point.

When I came home from the Blue Moon with the news that I had been hired, my mother worked hard to contain her enthusiasm. She was so wary of me in those days. She looked up at me from the sofa, where she sat fanning herself in the heat, as I mumbled that I had gotten the job. She started to exult—she had actually succeeded in doing me a favour—and then caught herself. "Well, that's fine, son."

My first full day of work, she came by with the bagged lunch that I had forgotten on the kitchen table that morning. She chatted with Mr. Sigrun by the cash register as I unloaded a new shipment of *Shower Room Shenanigans* and winced.

When I got home she asked me over iced tea what I thought of the place. I screwed up my face and shut my eyes, protesting the question: *"I don't know, Mom."*

"I guess it would be your father you would speak to about those things," she conceded—imagining perhaps that we did something out in the shop other than stare fixedly at balsa wood and fibreglass laminates.

When my mother met my father he was still in dentistry school and she was teaching in a one-room school north of Dundurn, Saskatchewan. She told me a hundred times when I was growing up that you have to look for men like my father with a flashlight, seeing in his reticence and disposition to preoccupation an enduring and charming strength. My father, possessing the emotional vocabulary of a miniature plastic barnyard animal, would leave the room.

My father and I began eating lunch together at the Riverside Grill, an Arborite-and-aluminum diner located in the mall. Over BLTs and as I listened to accounts of root canals gone awry and rot gone right through to bone, I decided two things: I could not be my father, and I would floss and brush vigorously every remaining day of my life.

In the late afternoon, when I got off work, I would sit in my father's waiting room until he finished with his last patient and drove us home. He usually ran late, and his receptionist, Rachel Freeman, and I would wait with our jackets on and make jokes about my father's difficulties with schedules. Mrs. Freeman was thirty-two and had worked for my father for two years. She had moved to Dunsmuir from the city when she married Roddy Freeman, who grew up down the road from us and always seemed to be hitting someone. When they split up she decided to stay in town because of the job she had gotten in my father's office. She said that getting that job was about the only luck she had had in the previous couple of years. When my father's last patient left, we would open the door. A minute later he would bound into the waiting room, apologizing. We would usher him out.

When the Perseid shower comes every summer, my father is distracted even beyond what is normal for him. For days beforehand he studies the weather map, praying for clear skies. The Perseid shower is caused by the collision of the earth with a cloud of dust from old comets that lies in the path of the earth's orbit. Every year, on the 15th of August or so, the night lights up with silent white streaks. For years, my mother and I sat there with him, watching.

We understood him to be more accessible than he was. We imagined that in loving him as we did, we gained a reliable knowledge of him. The meteor shower, we imagined, interested him because it was beautiful, or because it was unusual, or because it was fire made of burning ice, or something. His interests were as timid as he was, we surmised, and of course astronomy pleased him. He was drawn to odd small things that bordered on insignificance because that was how he was, as well. This was foolishness. To have lived beside him and have never grasped how he struggled with his life—it was a kind of ignorance that makes me twist now, thinking of it.

The last time we watched the meteors together I was seventeen. It was the warmest night that year; we sat out on the back lawn in our patio chairs with our clothes clinging to us like Saran Wrap on thawing bacon, perspiration beading on glistening white flesh.

Rachel sat beside my mother, and on Rachel's other side my father, then me. "And if you follow the pointer stars of Ursa Major, you come to Polaris . . . right . . . there." My mother and I listened idly. Rachel had never heard of the Galilean moons before; my mother and I, a thousand times. He was performing. Even in the heat his enthusiasm was enough to embarrass me.

It was the first time I understood it to be deliberate.

"And when these things were found, they completely shook the Aristotelian worldview, because they were a completely new thing. It suggested that the orthodoxy might be improved upon in some ways, that its account of the universe might conceivably be incomplete. What this meant for the Renaissance, for the rebirth of scientific inquiry, was . . ." And he waved his arms at all these things up there and I looked over at Mrs. Freeman and she was sitting up, staring first at Jupiter and then at my father, rapt. My mother got up and walked back to the house.

Nothing prepares me for a good meteor shower. A couple of falling stars every half hour, I think, no big deal. But some years it is much more than that, and I am never disappointed afterwards, although sometimes I expect to be. The beauty of the thing on a dark moonless night away from the lights of town is enough that you'd think that everyone would know about it and talk about it all the time. But they don't. And it happens anyway, without them.

After he died it took us a weekend to clean out his shop and turn the space into a second garage bay. The stuff in there was returned to the dump from where it had been gathered. By Saturday afternoon it was empty, and by noon Sunday we had finished cleaning and were painting. We even painted the concrete parking pad, with long-handled rollers that streaked across the floor in radiating and coalescing lines. When we were done, you'd have thought we had taken off the roof, the place was so much brighter.

That last year I watched the meteors with him, and saw my mother walk inside, I stared up at the sky, willing him to be happy, to be satisfied with what was before him. It was quiet for a long time and then I stood up, too, and went back to the house. At the side of the porch I stopped and looked up at the sky. My father was pointing out more astronomical minutiae. Rachel leaned close, listening intently. My father's voice fell away.

That year the shower began with a flash and suddenly a dozen white wakes were seared across the heavens. They appeared high above the western horizon and tracked down to the southeast, disappearing over the neighbours' barn almost before you could get a fix on them, and Rachel's gasp was caught in her throat. Then there were another half-dozen, higher up this time, and slower, moving mostly parallel to one another, like high-altitude aircraft flying in formation. It seemed incomprehensible that they should be so quiet; everything alive seemed to have stopped to watch the meteors. Even the distant highway was silent and the crickets were still, for the first time since the heat had arrived.

This was in 1981.

Carol was a hundred miles off the coast of Southampton Island, headed for Coral Harbour, when the wind came up. It was early in the year and it was still very cold. Ice hung from the rigging like great stalactites. She had wanted to make it out of Hudson Bay and into the North Atlantic before the autumn weather turned, and so she had left Churchill very early in the season. The ice pack had only begun to break up, and large pans still crowded together on the horizon. When the visibility began to worsen, she worried first about the ice.

As the wind mounted it became apparent that she would have to change course. The boat was pounding into the oncoming seas so hard she stopped entirely in the trough of each wave, and Carol briefly lost steerage as a consequence. As she turned the boat off the wind to run parallel with the sea, the boat's rolling increased dramatically. She was afraid that the boat might roll right over on her side, so she shortened sail, and it was a little better.

Then the wind mounted further and the rolling became more severe, even with the sails all but doused. It was only possible to head downwind, and downwind was the western shore of Hudson Bay. Carol was being driven toward a lee shore, and she was unable to alter course from it. She tried slowing her progress. She let out a long loop of anchor line, with spare sails and an anchor tied to it; she towed this apparatus, and it slowed her from six knots to three. She looked at the chart. It would take her twelve hours before she hit the lee shore.

All her life, she had felt a nearly constant urge to just launch herself from any height or off any boat. Once when she was pregnant she was on a ferry on Lake Huron and felt herself begin to lift up one foot. She fell back, nauseous with self-contempt and alarm.

She watched the knotmeter click along. She was twenty-five miles from shore, fifteen, ten. The wind had increased. She could see the low grey hills of

Kivalliq in front of her when she realized that, close in to shore, the wind had lessened. She tried turning and it worked. The wind had slowed enough that she could reach along parallel to the shore. She cut the line she was towing. She continued like this for another six hours, and then the wind fell abruptly and she rounded up further and made for Coral Harbour.

# HUDSON BAY, IN WINTER

The Harbour Hotel in Wager Bay, on the coast of Hudson Bay, had twenty-two rooms and a bar that smelled always of cigarettes and *muktuk*. *Muktuk* is whale skin and blubber. In the summer when the people are eating whale, not a room in any building in the hamlet is spared the smell. Kablunauks down south pride themselves on acquiring the taste for pungent Gorgonzola and for garlic—after a whale has been shot, the walls of the Harbour Hotel could be painted with a slurry of Gorgonzola and garlic and you'd think it pleasant, fashionably textured wallpaper.

A month after Mary arrived in Wager Bay, from Ottawa, fresh out of nursing school, she decided three things: she would join the Book-of-the-Month Club; Dan, her most-of-the-time boyfriend since high school, would have to do after all; and she would not allow herself to be this lonely again. Dan flew up the following summer to stay. She was making more money up there than both of them had together in the south. The first thing he said in the airport was "I smell fish."

Louisa was the janitor at the nursing station. She was nineteen years old and, apart from Mary, the only constant presence. Other nurses rotated through the place in a succession of flights from marriages gone abruptly awry and patterns of behaviour that required interruption. All these motivations generally gave way, pretty quickly, in the face of minus-fifty and isolation like a lockdown. Mary and Louisa ate lunch together at the Harbour Hotel twice a week, or more often, if Louisa was looking frustrated. Mary, ever the pragmatist, was prepared to eat any number of chiliburgers with Louisa, and listen to her problems forever, if it meant Louisa would keep coming to work. Each dreaded the other's vacations.

Louisa's son was Little Billy Tagalak, his father was Big Billy Tagalak and, in Mary's estimation, a big nuisance. "How is Little Billy, Louisa?"

"His cold is getting better. My mom says no smoking in the house until it's gone, so everyone is glad his nose isn't running so much."

"I'll have the pork chop, Maurice. And a cup of coffee."

"A chiliburger please. And a Coke."

"I think there's trouble between Billy and Marilyn Taluk these days."

"There's trouble wherever Billy goes."

Louisa nodded. "How's Dan, is he finding it better here?"

"Lately, yes. He's starting to meet people, to go out on the land and whatnot."

"He's a friendly guy, I guess. Likes meeting people."

"Yes."

"It's good."

Mary nodded. She drank her coffee and looked out the window at the forming blizzard. Out on the sea ice the blowing snow was already obscuring the horizon. The hunters would have to be just about in already, or they'd be stuck there and getting ready to pitch camp, to wait it out.

"Bronchiolitis will be getting going again soon."

"I have a feeling it won't be as bad this year."

"The fall has been quiet."

"As good as we could expect," Louisa said.

"Want any pie?" Mary asked.

"Sure."

Louisa had two brothers out there. The third had disappeared five years before. He was out on the sea ice and people thought he must have fallen through a crack during a storm, trying to get home. Everyone had looked for him for days, but had found nothing. Last year Tommy Toolik had been out trapping fox ten miles

inland and came upon his snow machine and picked-
over bones, no sign of what had happened. Everyone
was happy the bones were found. There were enough
ghosts wandering around the tundra as it was.

The nursing station was a brightly lit prefabricated
sheet-metal shed built atop a stone outcropping that
surveyed the whole settlement. Beside it was a twenty-
foot-tall granite Inukshuk that the federal government
gave the Kartuk brothers fifteen thousand dollars to
build, from the Community Heritage Monuments
Program. Whenever Jack Angoo, the member of parliament, visited, he was quizzed about whether he could
get any more monument money. Next year, he
promised, a life-size bowhead whale, with a little calf
too, maybe. The year after, maybe a granite ice cap.

The Toongies and the Tortooks were sitting in the
reception room waiting for their chest X-rays, part of
the TB survey. Louisa went into the X-ray room to
warm up the equipment. Mary was scheduled to do the
well-woman clinic after lunch, and she grinned at
Ophelia Sateanna and slipped her rings into her pocket
as Ophelia, with less enthusiasm, rose and smiled.

The arrangement was that a woman came in on the
Thursday of the week of her birthday; twenty
Sagittariuses in a row would wear anyone down. When
Mary walked into the little laboratory with a stack of
pap smear slides, at first she didn't even notice Louisa

standing there, and when she did, she saw that Louisa was looking at a pregnancy slide test and was weeping.

She walked over to Louisa and put her arm around her and looked down at the slide and the little magenta + sign on it.

"Oh Lou, look, you have lots of choices here. Don't get overwhelmed."

"Mary," Louisa said.

"Yes?"

Louisa ran out of the lab and put on her parka, leaving the front door swinging open and minus forty blowing in like an open meat freezer.

The festival that celebrates the founding of the town by whalers and priests is held in early winter. In the beginning, the people profited through their interaction with these men: the hunters were paid members of the whaling crews; the tools they brought home—steel sewing needles, rifles, shotguns, sharpening stones, and axes—made their lives easier but not fundamentally different. Some of the hunters became leaders of the Kablunauks' whale hunt, honoured for their ability to find the whale pods, and to handle the small boats that chased down the bowheads and the rights and the smaller, stranger narwhals. The people had stayed alive for millennia hunting the whales from tiny skin boats, and they knew what was knowable of them. This was a proud time for the people, in their dealings with the

Kablunauks; there was a version of mutual respect then that has not been sustained.

Today, to the extent that Kablunauks are interested in the people, they are interested in features of their lives that were abandoned thirty years ago: the famine, the *iglu*, slavery, whaling from the *qayaq*, song cousins. No one knows how to answer the questions that people from the universities are always asking.

Shrug. It sounds like it must have been very cold a lot.

Kablunauks seem not to understand that the history of the Inuit is contained in what they are. Kablunauks wish to buy soapstone carvings of men in sealskin trousers spearing seals as a way of capturing that tradition, unconscious that the people never carved stone ornaments before the Hudson's Bay Company paid them to. They were nomads, and carried what they owned over the tundra. Heavy ornaments had a limited place in that life.

Around the prefabricated government buildings, disposable diapers poke through the shifting snowdrifts, plastic bags from the Hudson's Bay store fly like aerial jellyfish through the streets, and the unmarked tundra beyond looks more and more alien to everyone.

The day before the festival is Dog Day. Feral dogs run in the garbage dump and on the periphery of the town; it is a problem in every Arctic community. Every year children are mauled, sometimes killed and eaten. On Dog Day all the dogs that belong to anyone are tied up.

Beginning at noon any dog that is not tied up is shot. The teenagers enjoy this. The carcasses are burned by the ocean with gasoline. The smell is like tires burning.

Mary stepped into the night and held the door for Dan. They were on their way to the Hamlet Dance, the first night of the festival. It was perfectly black and the stars glared like electric arcs. Dan closed the door behind them and they both shuddered and hunched their shoulders. They were going to be late for the dance because Dan had not been home when Mary got back from the clinic. He had been visiting one of the old men, he said, seeing if there might be any work helping to run someone's trapline. He had stopped talking about getting a government job. In the hurried dressing for the dance he added that he was starting to think that he might be able to live up here, you know, over the long run.

They turned to walk into the wind to the community centre.

"Who?" she asked, through her hood.

"What?"

"Which one of the men?"

"The one we always say hi to at the Hudson's Bay store."

"Apulardjuk."

"Yes."

They walked on, squeaking over crystalline snow.

At the dance a table had been laid out, covered with pots of *muktuk* and *iviaq*. The walrus smelled almost as strongly as the whale, and on entering the hall it was as if one were being pushed facedown in entrails. Laughter boomed out through tobacco smoke and steam; the overhead lights shone down in broad purple cones.

The hall was a Quonset hut dating from the war, made of galvanized steel and floored with plywood. Bright industrial lights hung from the ceiling, trying their best to penetrate the smoke in the air. There were five hundred people packed into the little building.

Louisa sat with Little Billy on her lap against one wall. Her mother was standing not far away. Louisa waved Mary and Dan over to sit with her. Lined up against one wall were chairs borrowed from the school for the elders. A dozen of the older men and women sat on these too-small hard-backed chairs, their sealskin *kamiks* shining in the electric light, bright skirts draped over blue jeans and bountiful laps.

Louisa's father, Simionie Ooluk, sat with his drum among the old people, smoking his pipe at the end of the row. Simionie Ooluk was one of the few elders whom Mary didn't know. He was on no regular medications, and the only time she had seen him in the clinic was when he had come in with an infected cut in his hand. He had sewn it up when he was out on the land, he said, and had used cotton thread. He had done a reasonable job. Mary had given him some antibiotics and, in an effort to win his approval, several packages of sterile suture material for the next time, which he had accepted. Even after this he had not acknowledged her when they had seen one another in the Northern Store, ignoring her cheerful *kahn-a-weepie*, which from anyone else elicited at least a nod and a smile. Her first impression was that he didn't like Kablunauks, or maybe it was a gender thing, but long after she had stopped greeting him, she noticed that his interaction with the other Inuit proceeded along the same lines. He moved through them like a sled dog. Everyone kept well out of his way, would move aside if he was coming but would not interrupt their conversation or vary their gaze. He sat straight and silent and wore a thin wispy beard in the fashion of the old men. He still hunted with dogs.

Mary watched him for a long time and he did not move. She looked over at Dan, who was smiling across the room at someone Mary couldn't see.

Mary said, "How are you, Louisa?"

Louisa said, "A little better, maybe."

"Things will be okay."

Dan started laughing and then, looking back at his girl-friend and Louisa, choked it into his hand. Mary looked through the dark and smoky room but didn't see who Dan had been looking at. Louisa excused herself, dumped Little Billy off her lap and walked into the crowd.

It was only in the late sixties that the last of the families came in off the land in the Keewatin District. Even these holdouts had been deeply affected by contact—rifles, pots and pans, matches, Coleman stoves—long before coming into town, but think about this: thirty-five years ago there were still families listening to mid-winter storms in houses of packed snow. For many of the young men and women it is still normal to think of the night and the wind as malevolent and lethal.

The visitor finds this place more familiar than unfamiliar. The rooms are just as warm and dry here as in the south, the television works the same way, the bathtubs are as comfortable. The tundra is marvelled at, as is the view from the airplane descending to the airport. On the walk between the airport and the taxi, it really is cold outside. Really cold.

A few months later and the visitor is struck by how similar her life up here is to that of her new friends. Chiliburgers at the Harbour Hotel, videos and Cheez Doodles on weekend nights. During the festival everyone tries to build an *iglu* and mostly the *iglus* fall in. The hunters ride snowmobiles and carry hand-held satellite receivers to guide their way home. Ask, and you can go with them. You can drive into the middle of the caribou herd yourself and shoot these docile and imbecilic creatures, shoot as many as you feel like skinning. The barriers between the people are not in what is done, or how. Not anymore.

The drumming started and the talk died away. Simionie Ooluk spun his drum and began singing a song about the woman shapeshifter, Sedna, who has the body of a fish and who hangs out by the floe edge, trying to lure hunters into the water. Mary had heard this song before, had had it explained to her, how once the hunter was in the water Sedna's fingers became fish and her teeth were as sharp and pointed as a seal's so that she could dismember him with one bite. Mary had listened to these stories and the other savage accounts of the spirit world and its interaction with the world of man with awe and disgust; walking through the frigid night, the dark low hills barely visible under the moon, she had wondered why, with a life as hard as these people's, they needed a spirit world so hostile and unforgiving. But then she realized how naive that question was, and suspected that she had answered it in her own framing of the question. So what did that mean then? There was no warmth to be had in this place, even in an interior landscape? What refuge existed in the snow and wind?

Simionie stamped his feet and sang louder, his nasal, high-pitched growl hopping through a cadence of fear; everyone listened, and sat straight in their chairs. The old men and women did not smile and held their mouths tightly and grimly. Simionie sat down, and for a moment there was no movement or noise. Then conversation slowly returned to the room, the young people first, then stepwise by generation, progressively older. Simionie's drum was between his knees and he looked like he was asleep.

Mary looked around at the room, examining people for their reactions to Simionie's song. Dan was watching a woman smoking a cigarette. The new librarian, Mary figured. Her eyes were so blue Mary could see their colour across the room. The librarian quickly looked away. Louisa sat down beside Mary and looked over at her father, still apparently napping, and then back to Mary. Simionie shifted in his chair and Louisa's eyes darted back to him. He settled again, and she looked back at Mary, relieved. Mary lifted her eyebrows. Louisa shrugged.

Big Billy showed up as the throat singing started. The two women singers sat cross-legged, facing one another. Their polytonal and discordant harmonies rose above them and filled the room. Billy was drunk and friendly. As he crossed between the audience and the singing women he did a little step dance. There were a few laughs. He bowed to the audience. The women continued singing. If they were aware of him they did not show it. Billy stepped to the side. He walked up to Louisa. He did not acknowledge Mary. "Hello, Billy," Louisa said, in English. He replied in Inuktitut.

"You missed my father's song," Louisa continued.

"Good."

Billy nodded at Dan. Dan nodded back. After a moment he turned and walked away. The throat singers finished. People clapped quietly. One of the young men plugged in the PA and "Pump Up the Jam" began throbbing into the hall. The kids all stood up and began dancing in their sealskin boots.

Toward midnight Billy appeared again on the dance floor, much drunker now. The old people watched the dancing from the sides, tapping their feet and smiling, talking to the young people who came over to visit. Billy seemed to prompt no response at all. Mary and Dan tried dancing but then they stopped and sat down in their chairs, perspiring, and frozen. Louisa was still sitting and watching. Mary smiled at her. Then she looked again and suddenly Simionie was kneeling on the floor and talking in Louisa's ear. Billy stumbled toward them and pulled on Louisa's arm. Simionie stood up and said something to Billy. Billy blanched. Everybody nearby looked suddenly embarrassed and stared at the floor. Simionie took Louisa by the arm and led her away. She followed her father silently. Billy sat down on the floor.

It is difficult for a Kablunauk to know the extent to which magic survives, because anyone who would know will not speak of it. Nurses spend twenty years in a community and remain mostly ignorant of these matters. They know all the other secrets—the incests and the different betrayals and the madnesses. And they know that there are clearly men and women who are avoided and feared. But it is possible to fear for very non-mysterious reasons too. They find that the intersection between magic and the more familiar gods of sex and loneliness and selfishness is far larger and more complete than they ever would have suspected before they came here and saw magic at work.

Three in the morning and so cold the snow squealed under Constable Lucien Gregoire's stamping feet. Mary woke slowly to the hammering on her door. Her eyes were still red from the fighting before they had gone to bed. The constable did not say anything at first when Mary opened the door. He stepped inside. The blast of cold swirled around her nightie. He wanted her to come and see Billy Tagalak. Billy was drunk, and waiting outside the nursing station. "Lucien," she said, "this isn't anything new, I don't know what I'm supposed to do for him." But she was already pulling a sweater on and reaching for her boots.

Dan looked out from the bedroom. He said, "Hello, Lucien." Lucien nodded at him. Mary told Dan that she was going into the nursing station. "Don't go anywhere," she added. Dan just looked at her. Mary and the Mountie bustled out into the cold.

Billy had phoned Lucien at home and asked if he would get the nurse for him. It was an emergency, he had said, and he would meet them there. Someone was going to get hurt, he said, and wouldn't elaborate.

Their lungs ached with the first breath of the night air. Constable Gregoire walked quickly toward the nursing station and Mary followed him as fast as she could. She fell steadily farther behind. The snow was so cold her feet slid with every step and she almost fell, over and over again.

At the nursing station Constable Gregoire stopped at the locked door and looked around the frozen blackened night. "Mary, he isn't here."

"I guess he decided to go to sleep, Lucien. We don't really know that anything is wrong, do we?"

"From the tone of his voice I think we should go and see."

Mary sighed. "Okay." It was almost four in the morning now.

They knocked on Billy's door. There was no answer. Lucien turned the knob and they went inside. They lit a kerosene lamp and kicked aside garbage as they walked through his house. His CD player was on repeat, playing Johnny Cash. Empty Export A cigarette packages were everywhere. Half the kitchen table was covered by foil laboriously rubbed onto the Formica. On the wall above the kitchen sink was a picture of Jesus on a piece of plywood and finished in high-gloss Varathane. The bed was unmade and the mattress was covered with amber oval stains interlaced together. One of Louisa's dresses lay on the floor.

At Simionie's house only his wife, Winnie, was home. She didn't know where anyone was, she said. Louisa's boy was peering from the kitchen, silently. Lucien addressed the step, ashamed that he was embarrassing this old woman. The dogs were gone. Billy's snow machine was not around, although tracks circled the house. There were also dogsled tracks leading away. Overtop them, snow-machine tracks.

The last famine was only forty years ago. One year the caribou abruptly changed their migratory path and the hunters waited at the usual river fords and for weeks and months saw only the little ground squirrels, the *sik-siks,* and the geese, flying far overhead. It is not clear what precipitated this. Certainly the caribou population had not diminished greatly, for a few years later they were as plentiful as ever, and back in their usual calving and feeding grounds, but for four years they could not be found, vanished in the tundra far away from the people.

Until the famine happened the people had maintained a middle path with the Kablunauks. They had remained on the land, and were self-sufficient, but they bought the rifles and tents and Coleman stoves with pride and pragmatism. If these things were not available, they knew, it would have been harder, but they could have coped.

When the famine was at its worst, the people were too weak to build cairns for the dead. They did as well as they could, and dragged the bodies out onto the tundra and stacked what rocks they could lift onto them. In short order, foxes and dogs got into most of these, and the cracked and bleached bones of children and old people may be seen on the periphery of the inland hunting camps. Around and among them, small and pitiful clumps of rocks sit, as gestures.

With the famine came the end of the people's time on the land. In another era, with the return of the caribou, babies would be born, and the people would learn once again of their resilience, but this time they moved into the villages that the government built for them. Airplanes and ships brought in tins of corned beef. When the caribou returned the people were only pleased. It was good, but it did not matter as much.

Simionie's tent was pitched in a small valley, and recognizable for miles, for its many years' worth of patchings. The sled, the *qomotik*, was carefully stood on edge beside the tent. Rock and snow were all around. Lucien and Mary approached slowly on the RCMP snow machine and shut off the engine. The tent was motionless and silent. The dim early-morning light seemed to absorb the sound.

Inside the tent there was blood pooling on the canvas floor. A sleeping bag lay against one wall, with the outline of a body within. The lamp was still burning. Small plastic bags of mosses and grasses spilled out beside the lamp. A caribou antler sat beside the lamp, on the floor, in the blood. There was weeping from the sleeping bag, like gravel shaking, worn out and exhausted. A Coleman stove was burning, and there was a pot of foul-smelling tea boiling on one of the burners, clumps of moss and grass, like floating hair, roiling in the pot. Louisa sat up, not recognizing either of them; the bloody sack between her legs swung like a yo-yo when she tried to stand and then she fell. Mary laid Louisa back down in the sleeping bag. She whispered to her to keep still.

Beside the tent the dogs were feasting. The old man's rifle was nearly covered in snow. It had been lying there since it had fallen out of his mouth. A parabola of bone and blood stretched out over the snow. The dogs growled and fought with one another. There was the sound of clothes ripping.

Billy's tracks circled the tent and came no closer to the body than thirty feet. Over the horizon, leading away from town, his still-fresh tracks were disappearing in the rising wind.

This was in 1997.

The freight comes by rail to Churchill and is then loaded onto barges during the brief shipping season, for transport to the little hamlets of Kivalliq. For most of a century, Churchill has been the supply depot for this part of the Arctic. Because of this relationship, there is a sense of commonality between Churchill and the little Inuit towns upcoast. People know of one another. Women go to Churchill to deliver their babies, and become familiar with the people who live there. The nurses in Kivalliq call Churchill for help when things go very badly.

The schoolteacher's disappearance was therefore discussed in those little towns. Mary and Daphne each learned of it and wondered what she had wanted. More isolation? They had heard the story of her husband's death, and interpreted that in a limited and clinical manner. Something about pathological grief responses. They had no idea what the old woman would want in the bush with winter imminent.

By the following spring she still had not returned to town and there had been no word from her. It was May and the river ice was going soft. It was no longer safe to travel and would not be again until the ice was out. Everyone seemed quick to conclude that she was dead.

# STARLIGHT, STARBRIGHT

When a regiment of the Canadian army is in the field, it uses a system of nicknames to refer to its components over the radio net, in order to shorten broadcast times. Aerial reconnaissance becomes Hawk Eye; military police, appropriately, becomes Strong Arm; intelligence becomes, less plausibly, Ponder Box. The medical support elements of a combat regiment are Starlight, suggesting, perhaps, the cool soothing illumination that a soldier in the mud might long for.

The battle school of the Royal Canadian Artillery is in the southwestern corner of Manitoba. This is short-grass prairie: thin sandy soil, languorous pool halls, and lots of squint-eyed understatement. Cattle country partly, and away from the hills there is wheat, sunflower, and barley. Towns every forty miles or so—a Chinese food restaurant, a bar, a garage. Spend a month out here and you'd need a reason why.

On the base, the hills are pocked and divoted by half a century of field artillery exercises. The army is different from the farmers; the farmers neither like nor understand the soldiers and the money they waste. To the farmers, the army is a part of the country that doesn't make sense. The army is from Toronto and from Newfoundland, and a distressingly large part of it comes from Quebec. Montreal, even—Captain Joly, the regimental medical officer, had drunk *café au lait* on tree-lined boulevards and read that day's *Le Monde* among men and women sinuous and sleek. None of whom could imagine this place even in their worst nightmare. Try to describe it to them and they just look at you and ask how you allowed yourself to wind up in such a place anyway.

The thing is, he would have told them, he told himself as he drove to work every morning, if you give a blank cheque to somebody, you shouldn't be surprised when they cram as many zeroes onto the thing as they can before cashing it. While still in medical school, Joly, anticipating imminent affluence, developed a taste for expensive clothes and restaurant meals. He ran up his credit cards until he was entirely insolvent and about to be evicted, so he signed up with the army; they paid for books and tuition, and gave him a salary—he agreed to work for the military wherever it wanted him, for three years. The recruiting guy talked about Cyprus or Germany or even the base right there in Montreal, and Joly had nodded eagerly. "When does the salary start?"

he had asked. All the zeroes added up to southwestern Manitoba. *"Tabernacle,"* he had said over and over again as he drove west staring at the flat black-and-green fields that never seemed to end.

Along with the battle school, the base quartered the Third Regiment of the Royal Canadian Horse Artillery. In the regiment there were four hundred men and a half-dozen women between the ages of eighteen and forty. If any of them had any significant medical problems they wouldn't have been posted to the regiment— combat readiness and all that. Joly's responsibilities fell to applying ice to twisted ankles, putting a cast on the occasional broken fist, and prescribing tetracycline, admonishment, and condoms to embarrassed young men. He was finished work most days by 9:30 a.m. and spent the remainder of the morning listening to the radio and reading the newspaper. In the afternoons he slept on his examining table. In the evenings he sat alone in the library of the officers' mess and wrote letters home. At night he dreamed often of the ocean and of the mountains. Standing before the mirror in the mornings he would shut his eyes trying to preserve the flaming iridescent colours of the night before. Some days he would pass the whole morning at his desk motionless, with his eyes shut and his hands folded on the desk in front of him. The medics worried about him continually.

Great efforts were made to make Joly feel a part of the military fraternity. Functions were held at the officers' mess on a weekly basis. They were for the most part obligatory-attendance affairs and Joly would mingle to the extent required. The medics at the hospital were instructed to call for him at the slightest provocation. "The least little thing," he would emphasize.

"Gotcha, boss," they would reply. Suspicions grew, in the minds of those sober enough to keep track, that it was not pure chance that the only work he did most weeks was during the commanding officer's anecdote about the pilot, the 155mm round, and the zucchini.

At these gatherings, two groups formed that were utterly insoluble in one another. The regimental officers fancied themselves the real army, the Reason You Are Here. (Joly raised his eyebrows at that.) The base officers were mostly sensible men and women with legitimate skills—engineers, accountants, that sort of thing—who had found themselves with families and limited options and no choice but to ride out their time until they got posted somewhere with a movie theatre within an hour's drive. Both of the groups were baffled by the other. Joly was baffled by everybody, of course. But only until his beeper went off, and then you couldn't catch him with a radar gun.

Monique Lefevre was seventeen and from the Magdalen Islands in the Gulf of St. Lawrence. When she graduated from high school she asked her friends what they were going to do. Mostly, they shrugged. There were a few who planned to move to Montreal or Quebec City and there were a few more who were going to get married that summer, but on the whole, her friends had the same problem she did, the same problem anyone has who comes from a small place with few jobs and no roads out: she could leave and be a long way away and lonely until she had made a new home someplace else and was changed irrevocably, or she could stay home and smoke cigarettes in the coffee shop with her friends and be very bored, at least until she was so bored that she generated her own problems to preoccupy her until she was old.

She saw an advertisement on the television about the military. "Be all that you can be," it said. The idea had never occurred to her. She phoned the toll-free number and they sent her a plane ticket to the recruiting station in Quebec City. She wrote an exam and showed them her high school transcript. There was some consternation, as she did not qualify for any of the technical trades. She had not taken physics or chemistry, and her reading comprehension had not shown itself well in their little test. They asked her if she liked the outdoors. Sensing their hopes, she said yes. They asked her if she was interested in a non-traditional occupation. Again, she said yes. She asked if she couldn't be a clerk, or an electrician. They said no, not according to her aptitude test. She asked if she could write it again. They said no. It had taken a day and a half just to get there from the

Magdalen Islands. In the cubicle next to the one she was in there was a just-graduated medical student receiving his first posting.

Monique Lefevre arrived in Manitoba in January, in time for basic training. This was the height of bad luck. But Manitoba is where basic training for the artillery is done, for francophone and anglophone artillery soldiers alike, and this was the next available course. As the bus from Winnipeg pulled into Shilo, 110 miles removed from even that slim piece of civilization, Lefevre pushed her forehead against the glass and stared. The glass was intensely cold, and when she leaned back from it again her forehead was white and numb.

She and the others were greeted at the bus exit by a man clad in a green parka and wind pants that made him look like Bonhomme Carnaval dipped in paint. He shouted in one long exhalation that they were welcome in Shilo, that the francophones should line up here, the anglos there, that it was very late at night and they would be shown to their rooms, questions would have to wait until morning, answer when I call your name, *réponds quand j'appelle ton nom*, Jean Claude Alois, James Astwood . . .

From the window of her room Lefevre could see down the road behind the barracks. The snow was plowed into drifts nine feet high. The few vehicles moving—a pizza delivery car, a military police car on patrol—were visible only when immediately across from the building. They seemed to emerge from within the snow, rumble and squeak along the road, and then disappear into it again, as if they were whales coming up for air. There was winter in the Magdalens but it was nothing like this.

In the morning they began running. They ran from the mess hall to clothing stores to the orderly room to the gymnasium. From the movies she had seen, she had expected much worse. And much better-looking men than these: the other students were from every small town from Jonquière to Smithers. They were not the bright lights of any society they had ever belonged to; this was evident in the glances around the room, the mutual deference, and the clumsy conversations. They were all between seventeen and twenty-two and there was enough acne between them to keep any number of skin-scrub salesmen happy for life.

Her roommate was Carole Lévesque, who was from Jonquière and spoke almost no English whatever and was not at all certain how she had wound up here, but had decided to ride it out and see where it led her. She chatted on and on about her boyfriend, Réal, back in Jonquière, and how the first leave she was given, she would fly back to see him, or maybe he would come here, they would hole up in a hotel in Winnipeg for a week, or, if they gave it to her, two weeks. Monique listened to this as she lay on her back on her bunk and wondered just how hysterical Carole would get and how long it would take.

The rest of that week was filled with all of them getting issued their gear and with sorting out the administrative blunders that had put three prospective F-18 mechanics on the same base as these woebegone artillerymen. Artillerypeople. The aircraft-mechanics-to-be extricated themselves with relief and said goodbye to the hollow-eyed recruits who were scheduled to go into the field the following week, thirty-two below and wind like a power tool. Their bus pulled away and Lefevre watched it go and decided to walk across the street to the gas station, where there was a pay telephone that you could talk on with some expectation of privacy. She thought her father would be wondering how she was doing by now.

When Joly met Monique Lefevre she lay weeping on a stretcher, in the arms of Carole Lévesque. She had bruises on both her cheeks, mud pressed into her oily blond hair, and dried blood at the side of her mouth. *Soldat* Carole Lévesque knew little about her except that she had been homesick and had sneaked out to use the phone and had been found outside the sergeants' and warrant officers' mess screaming in the snow with her trousers around her knees. A military policeman sat in a chair outside the examining room.

The nurse on duty, Lieutenant Ridgeway, concluded what she knew of the story with a snort. "Some asshole from the regiment, I guess. Fuckers should all be locked up."

"Do we know if penetration took place?" Joly asked.

"No, we don't."

"I guess I'm going to have to do swabs."

"I guess you are."

"Did you get the rape kit?"

"It's right here."

"Jeez."

"Let's get this over with, poor thing shouldn't have to lie here all night."

"No, she shouldn't."

Joly stepped outside the examining room to take a breath of air and to wash his hands. As he opened the door, Lieutenant Ridgeway turned to the girl. "Okay, private, we're going to have to get you into this gown now. There you go. Here, you can cover yourself with this."

The "assault kit" was an attempt by the military police to ensure that all necessary evidence was gathered by the doctor. The attacker's pubic hair, bite marks, and ejaculate all linger after him for at least a short while and, if recorded, may make the difference between a conviction or not. The post-assault assessment took about an hour to perform and included combing, swabbing, photographing, and sketching.

About ten of the victim's pubic hairs were required as well. Plucked, not cut.

Joly stepped back into the room, his hands shining pink. He put on a pair of sterile gloves. *"Il faut que je vous examine,"* he said apologetically to the young weeping woman.

*"Comment?"* she said to her friend.

"She doesn't consent, doctor," Lieutenant Ridgeway said.

"There's no way he'll be convicted if she doesn't let me examine her."

*"Il faut qu'il t'examine,"* Carole said to her friend, stroking her face.

*"Non, non, non,"* Lefevre said, rolling away toward the wall.

Joly sat down in the one remaining chair. Then to Lefevre: "If you want to stay here tonight I can admit you." Lefevre made no audible reply. Lévesque stroked her back. Ridgeway chewed her lip.

A week later, at a follow-up appointment, Lefevre sat in her chair staring at the floor.

"If you want to proceed with the charge it's never too late. Of course, you'd have to tell them who did it."

No answer.

"I know these combat arms guys can be pretty intimidating, but you can put this guy away if you want. He'd never be able to get at you again."

No answer.

"Do you have any vaginal discharge or pain upon urination?"

Outside you could hear the wind slamming some door someplace. It seemed to go on forever.

For Lefevre the winter passed like she was on a motorized treadmill that dragged her along in a precisely choreographed minuet of tedium and routine. She passed whole days where it seemed to her that she hadn't had a conscious thought. She could have returned to the Magdalens but there she would have had unlimited time to sit in that damn coffee shop and stare out at the snow. So she stayed on the base and polished her boots every night until nine and then she went to sleep and arose at five. The drill staff thought highly of her, but for obvious reasons—no one wanted to single her out, or even look her in the eye for that matter—the award for top recruit went to a speckle-faced boy from Saskatoon who could do eighty-four push-ups in a row without stopping. They took their places in the regiment in mid-March and Carole's boyfriend never did show up and Monique's predictions were wrong, there were no histrionics at all.

In the spring they deployed a thousand miles to the west, to Alberta. There a small detachment continued up to the Kicking Horse Pass, where it set up its guns under the direction of civilian forest rangers and fired rounds into the glaciers, setting off small avalanches in order that very large ones might be averted. This had been one of the regiment's duties for fifty years. It was called Av-Con, for avalanche control.

*Soldats* Lefevre and Lévesque were among those assigned to Av-Con; the remainder of the regiment stopped two hundred kilometres south of Calgary. It would spend the rest of the summer there, engaged in field exercises on the badlands.

For those soldiers sent up to the mountains, the spring was hallucinogenically strange. For officers and senior NCOs the task was a rebuke, an indication that they were thought to be unpromising commanders. Generally, the junior lieutenants would spend the mornings reading the want ads in the newspaper. Every military convention eroded out from under the watchful eyes of the ambitious and longtime-indoctrinated. In the morning the privates would emerge from the cabins they slept in, walk across the street to the one open-all-year café, and order breakfast. Out the windows of the Horseshoe Café the mountains could be seen shining silver and bright. At times it was almost as beautiful as the Magdalen Islands, and many days passed for Lefevre in which she was perfectly content. The waitresses at the café came to know the soldiers by name and soon it was as if they were residents. When heavy snow came, the soldiers knew that they would likely be called to roll out their guns and unpack the shells, but even this was welcome and pleasant work with a usefulness utterly unknown in usual military life. There were no concerns about camouflage nets or counterbattery fire. Leisurely and carefully, coordinates and gun settings were called out. Three or four or five rounds were fired, the whole valley rang with the explosions, and then there was a dull rumble. The avalanches were watched carefully through telescopes, to see that they did not extend to the slopes above the gun positions, and then more coffees were ordered at the Horseshoe Café.

Most days Lefevre slipped away from the town to sit on a tree stump she had found where the whole valley was stretched out before her. She could see the CN trains rumbling along the track, and elk, one by one, crossing open areas, stopping to paw at the snow and snort in the frigid crystalline air. They seemed to her unreasonably beautiful animals. Even from that distance their bearing and grace were excessive.

Lefevre wondered that those creatures could stay alive in snow so deep as this. She wondered if they were ever caught in the avalanches she had helped set off. She realized that they probably were. Of course, there would be avalanches anyway, even if they didn't set them off, and this made her feel better.

Since she had arrived in the mountains, her mother had written to her. She had been thinking that maybe Monique should come home. She seemed different, over the telephone, since she had left. She shouldn't just remain there because she was afraid of quitting, if she didn't want to be a soldier. There wasn't any point in struggling against the world just for the sake of struggle. Lefevre found herself appalled by this statement of her mother's, but unable to reply to it directly. She wrote back and told her mother that she thought staying in the army was a very pragmatic thing to be doing. For one thing, there was the pension plan.

The exercise range at Suffield seems even more unremittingly huge than either the mountains or the base in Manitoba. Five hundred wild horses live there, and most of the surviving pronghorn antelope as well. There are sufficiently few trees that they are marked individually even on the smallest-scale maps. Park an ambulance out here, climb up on its roof to sunbathe, and it's as if the world falls away beneath you. All there is is sky. Every couple of mornings someone comes by with food. Those loaves of Wonder bread and eggs and sausages are the only evidence available that the medical section hasn't been forgotten entirely. The radio crackles and hums but nobody calls for Starlight. Starlight awakes at irregular intervals with drool dripping onto the roof of the ambulance, wondering where he is.

The regimental aid station was the only portion of the regiment that knew such peace; the gun batteries split apart on arrival, like an angry family, and spent the whole spring charging about the range in their self-propelled howitzers as if in amphetamine-induced agitation. The staccato thump of sod, blown high into the air, never let up, even for a moment, and after a while it sounded like the wind, or surf, maybe—inaudible until it was listened for. The soldiers driving the ammunition trucks followed the guns around with maps taped to their dashes; they drove a steady circuit from supply point to gun emplacement, sleeping only when the trucks were being loaded or when, mercifully, they broke. The mechanics spent day and night repairing the disassembling machinery and the cooks travelled back and forth thirty and forty kilometres between the to-be-fed and the supply points. Nevertheless, as vigorous as the training might be, the effects of incoming artillery fire could not be sanely duplicated and the only casualties the medics saw were exhaustion and sprained ankles. A couple of snakebites. Dehydration, heat stroke. Just enough work to keep Docteur Joly from achieving total union with the roof of his ambulance.

Artillery rounds differ from one another in both the size and the nature of the projectile: the size is strictly a function of the gun doing the firing, but even for any given gun there was a diabolic array of options for the battery commander. Mostly, they fired off high-explosive rounds, for reasons of economy and the fact that it was easy to see them hit (because of all the sod in the air), and that made it easy to tell how close or how far you were from your target. But also available were illumination rounds, which lit up the night sky in a dull crump of eerie blue-green flare light, descending by miniature parachute onto the flammable prairie below. And white phosphorus, or Willie Pete, which erupted in a thousand streaking blazing shards outward from the impact crater, little clumps of burning pebbles which, it was said, burrowed into flesh like a dentist's drill. Really, more of a morale buster than anything else—couldn't penetrate even light armour, after all. And finally, there was the beehive round. This one was structured like a conical honeycomb made out of steel—at the core of the round was a charge of high explosive and in the compartments in the honeycomb sat ten thousand steel darts with razor-edged wings. The artillerymen spoke in awed tones of this device—takes the kill radius out to two hundred metres, the danger radius to four hundred. Imagine it.

By late June the threat of avalanche had diminished and the detachment was returned to the regiment in the desert. *Soldats* Lévesque and Lefevre were not pleased by this development and anyone working with them knew this within minutes of their arrival. Joly considered approaching Lefevre to see how she was doing, but decided against it. To make that kind of fuss—having her brought over from thirty miles away—he'd have to be more than curious, he decided. Anyway, she was always free to ask to see him. He talked the matter over with his sergeant, Roger Martin, who suggested he leave the matter alone. "Everyone gets over these things in their own way, doc," Martin said. "You can't go pushin' help on anyone."

Martin struck Joly as being one of the few sensible people he had met since joining the army. He had an understated reasonableness about him that left the doctor wondering what he was doing in the army in the first place. Joly decided to take his advice and not pursue the matter.

A couple of weeks later, the first real medical problem emerged in the form of one of the administrative clerks and an IUD-induced case of pelvic inflammatory disease, which was one of the possible complications, Joly remembered having explained when he put it in. Sergeant Martin and he had done the pelvic examination in the back of the platoon tent, and it was quickly clear that the clerk needed to be evacuated to the field hospital at brigade headquarters. It was the middle of the night and they were facing a thirty-mile drive over dirt track roads—easily an hour each way—and Sergeant Martin tightened his mouth as he radioed their intent to regimental headquarters. When he got off the radio he kicked the barracks box nearest to him so hard it cracked with a loud snap. Everyone in the tent turned to look at him. Martin walked into the back of the tent, where the woman lay on a cot. "Right then, soldier, you've got your way. Make sure your kit is packed. You'll

be leaving within the hour. And stop that whimpering."
Joly didn't know what his sergeant was carrying on
about. It was three in the morning and all he wanted was
what everyone wanted, to sleep.

Headquarters came back with permission to travel
and a safe route, which was to say a series of roads that
weren't being shelled at the time of their intended
travel. After dropping off the by-then vomiting clerk at
the field hospital, taking out the IUD, and writing some
admission orders for intravenous hydration and antibiotics, Joly and Sergeant Martin found a couple of
vacant stretchers in a storeroom and grabbed a couple of
hours' sleep. At breakfast they were standing in line waiting for eggs when Lévesque and Lefevre fell in behind
them. "Private Lévesque, Lefevre! How are things?" Joly
asked. The two women interrupted the conversation
they were having and blinked at them.

*"Très bien, merci, monsieur,"* Lévesque answered evenly.
Lefevre said nothing at all, staring straight ahead.
Sergeant Martin scooped his scrambled eggs onto his
plate and shuffled away down the line.

"Well, if you ever need anything, drop by the aid
post anytime, we always have coffee on," Joly said with
a smile that looked like it was propped up with little
twigs.

"Yessir," Lefevre finally answered.

"Okay then, take care now." He turned and followed
in the wake of Sergeant Martin.

When Joly caught up to the sergeant he was already half through his eggs and starting on his toast. "A word of advice, sir?"

"Sure."

"You know, you don't do them any favours when you talk to them like that in front of everybody. Those two already think they're special from everyone else in the regiment, and when other people see an officer being friendly the way you were, things get harder for them. See what I'm sayin'?"

"What a fucked-up organization this is."

"When is your time up, sir?"

"Two more years."

"Same as for them. You should try and make it go smooth as possible. The army can be pretty unsmooth sometimes."

The last three weeks of the deployment were reserved for the brigade commander's exercise. It was largely on their performance during this period that the battalion commanders were recommended for promotion: the chain of ambition and threat worked down to the battery and troop commanders and everyone knew that a good performance could salvage much and an incompetent one imperil everything. Everyone got a little insane as this time approached: Joly kept to himself, up on the roof of his ambulance. His tanning time was interrupted only by the daily, and sometimes twice-daily, briefings the colonel began giving the regimental officers. During these hour-long harangues under helmet, Joly mostly daydreamed. A few things he took in. Radio discipline and procedure was gonna fuckin' improve around here or heads were gonna start gettin' kicked. He took that in. And any forward observation officer who couldn't get fire on target within three corrections could look forward to a summer in cadet camp, wiping noses. And even the slightest deviation from safe procedure would result in charges laid. Is that understood? He got all that.

Which set off a whole new round of lectures from the battery commander. Doc, don't move the ambulance without talking to headquarters. Better yet don't move it at all, get one of the medics to do all the driving, someone who knows the firing schedule and how to get clearance from base. And finally: Access to live fire areas will be controlled by sentries. If you come upon a checkpoint, stop and find out if any changes to the firing schedule have been made. And follow their directions. They'll know the lay of the local area.

And then madness began. Joly was sleeping in the front seat of the ambulance, fully dressed, his knees against the dashboard, his chin tucked into his chest, when the packet of vehicles he was in started up as one and began to move. Four in the morning and they had been waiting at the rendezvous point for eight hours. His idea was, at least we're into the last of it now. I can't wait to get where we're going and set up camp again. A week later he was still sleeping with his knees against the dash of the truck, still wearing the same clothes, and still wondering when they were going to set up camp.

Sergeant Martin was driving with his forehead nearly on the windscreen, imagining that he could penetrate by proximity the vertical puddle that sat against the window, sloshed around by the ineffectual windshield wipers. His breath steamed against the glass and he would sporadically unroll his window and try to navigate with his head held out to the side, having forgotten perhaps the conclusion he had reached the last time, ten minutes previously, when he had attempted the same thing: fuck it's raining hard. Joly exhaled slowly and leaned against his own window, his head bouncing back and forth with the involuting road and then with a reverberating thump into the door.

"Jeez, sarge, what're you doing?"

"If you want to take over here, sir, be my guest."

"Do we know where we are?"

"Fuckin' rendezvous was supposed to be back three klicks, but there's nothing there. I have no fuckin' idea where we're supposed to be."

"Well, we're on the right road anyway, eh?"

No answer.

"Sergeant, please tell me we know what road we're on."

"Let's just keep going. We gotta come upon some-one, sooner or later."

Another hour, five kilometres and three deep-mud encounters later, they come to a crossroads and they stop and study the map. The doctor thinks he can see a line of hills through the rain, which would mean they were somewhere—there? The sergeant knows they are lost and is smoking his last dry cigarette, just staring, he's so mad. They're on strict radio silence but between the two of them they're thinking that maybe they should call someone. But what good would that do? Sure, we're reading you loud and clear. No, we don't have any idea where you are. Pause. Don't you?

From out of the night a rain-hooded face knocks on the driver-side window. Sergeant Martin unrolls it and recoils against the insurgent elements, the rain hood hollers something, "Where the fuck is the RV?" Sergeant Martin yells back.

The rain hood pushes some dripping blond hair to the side and hollers something more. Sergeant Martin leans forward trying to get a better look, the rain hood steps back and waves them forward.

"See, I told you we should just go straight," the doc-tor says.

No answer.

In the passenger mirror the slight figure in the green poncho stands on the road for a moment and then disappears in a gust of rain, Captain Joly and Sergeant Martin both watching in the mirror as the rain closes in around it.

Another five klicks and half an hour and this is clearly not the RV. *"Fuck. I have no idea and no cigarettes."* The rain falls even harder and the thunder crashes. Sergeant Martin pricks up his ears. That one was close.

*"That fucking bitch!"* Sergeant Martin throws the truck into reverse and turns it around. They're plowing through mud like a tugboat and the lightning begins— great radiant streaks erupting like daddy longlegs spiders off to the right and omigod the left. Sergeant Martin hollers into the radio: "Zero, this is Starlight: Cease fire! Cease fire!" And the passenger-side front tire collapses as hail falls all around in another thunder and they careen off into the ditch on the right, the truck tipping onto its side and stopping, the sergeant sitting on top of the doctor when things stop moving. "You okay, sir?"

"You're squishing me!"

The sergeant reaches above him and opens the driver-side door and begins to haul himself up and thunder again and nothing from the sky ever sounded like that: ten thousand shrieking steam whistles but thinner, briefer; and the sergeant falls back, now he's lying on top of the doctor. He bucks and he gasps, leaking warm ooze onto the man beneath him, and then with a shudder he stops.

This was in 1995.

Cora had lived in Pigeon River for four years before she finally decided to try it. She signed up for hunter's safety classes and bought herself a twenty-gauge shotgun. At first she went with the men she worked with at the clinic, and they showed her how to look for prairie chickens in the low branches of poplar trees and to wait until they had leaped and then to take a second before deciding whether or not to shoot.

She lagged behind them, to watch more carefully as they leaned into their shotguns and then fired. At their urging, she fired a few times, too, but she wasn't really trying to hit anything and she thought they sensed that.

Later, she went by herself, and studied the cut-barley fields carefully as she walked along. The first time prairie chickens rose up around her she was too startled to do anything except gasp. They were so much noisier when she was alone. And she was quieter, so she got closer.

The next time, she was prepared, and as she lifted the shotgun to her shoulder she saw the bird clearly and she swung the bead of the barrel through its path, and fired a little ahead of it, and it fell.

By the time the sun had begun to set she had four birds and she walked back toward her truck. She looked at the bloody little birds in her sack and looked away. She looked around at the swaths of cut grain and at the skeins of geese overhead and at her truck in the distance. It was where she was.

# MANITOBA AVENUE

... was a beautiful stretch of 1940s architecture that could have been buried in a tar pond, so perfectly preserved were its painted wood and stucco features. Shelly's Fabrics sat in all its lemon-yellow cheerfulness alongside the Riverside Grill, which shone with polished stainless steel and scrubbed Formica. Next was Dunsmuir Billiards, which had never, not for a moment, ever, shone with anything at all, but rather cast shadows within and without, even from the lights above the tables, and especially from Roddy Freeman, who sat in a debilitated and sullen mound behind the cash register, radiating anemic and unconvincing menace. The businesses of Manitoba Avenue had their own association, which met quarterly to discuss their declining fortunes, and to frame resolutions for the town council, to the effect that they were owed something, dammit, had been there long before all the highway strip malls and box stores had crept up over the last half-dozen years, and surely the town wasn't purposefully trying to destroy them? Roddy Freeman was the secretary-treasurer of the Manitoba Avenue Business Association and saw to it that these resolutions were published in the *Dunsmuir Post* each Tuesday, there to be read with inert sympathy by the townspeople, who, upon remembering which business he owned, wondered what he imagined they wanted their town to become. Or remain.

Across the street from the Riverside Grill and Dunsmuir Billiards was the Wagon Wheel, the bar of the employed. Jim remembered the place clearly, although it seemed to him he hadn't so often perceived it clearly—from the inside anyway—when he had lived here. The dim red light and a lax institutional character had never allowed for fastidious age-checking and he had spent most Saturday nights here in his final year of high school, affecting knowledge of the world and a fondness for rye whisky.

Rye. The elixir of the Canadian prairie. The place, all these places, came back to him with its taste. Rye and ginger, rye and Coke: rye, rye, rye. Lovely little word when you said it fast. Ice cubes and smoked-glass tumblers. He hadn't drunk rye or been back here in twenty years and hadn't thought of that time or this place in any detail since he moved to Toronto, to launch his career in retail plumbing and heating. This was the joke he planned to use at the reunion, which was scheduled for the weekend.

He sipped his glass of rye and ginger, which he had been nursing all night, and watched Country Music Television above the bar. Garth Brooks was pumping his fist in the air and singing the praises of love.

The decision to attend the reunion had unfolded quickly. Carol had left him the summer before, after their daughter had taken off. Brandy had found herself a Children's Aid Society worker who had placed her in about twenty different group homes for about an hour each, over the last year. He heard from her every few weeks, when she needed money. He gave her what she wanted, generally. Her mother was quickly emptying the bank account, too. It had turned into a race, between mother and daughter. Jim had adopted the posture of spectator, filling the account as quickly as it was emptied, by cashing in mutual funds and GICs. Come spring, he had taken out a second mortgage on the house and sold the car. Now that was gone. Apparently his wife was equipping a hardware depot in northern Manitoba somewhere. He was not particularly concerned about what either of them was doing with the money. When it ran out, which would be soon, it would be gone, and neither of them would have any further claim on him. Which would be a relief. He understood that this was an imperfect strategy for his complex family problems but it was the only one he had. Any endgame strategy, even a losing one, is better than none.

At least you have an idea how the whole business will conclude, he thought to himself.

Lovely Dunsmuir. He had visited his parents' graves. He had gotten a motel room in the Aloha Motel. He had watched late-night pornography in his room and had tried to decide whether the sex sounds coming through the walls were the real thing or a different channel. On the basis of the vibrations transmitted through the wall from the apposed headboard, he had optimistically concluded that they were the former, but the next morning an aging man in blue Manitoba Hydro overalls had left his room the same time Jim did and they exchanged looks of mutual assessment, envy being replaced by doubt in the space of two slow seconds.

His parents had died three years ago, one after the other in a sequence of malignancies. He had not attended the funerals. At the time he was in the basement, paralyzed with desperation, and when his sister called he had told her he couldn't get away from work. She didn't press him on the matter. They had not spoken since his mother's, the final, death. A little cheque followed in the mail a few months later. His sister had written a note, "Call if you have any questions." No signature. After that business Carol had given up on him. She had company.

The graves were well tended. He stayed about fifteen minutes and did not know what to think. He kept waiting for a surge of emotion to come over him, but the mosquitoes were biting him and there were other people in the cemetery, dropping off flowers. He bowed his head a little and looked respectful.

The invitation to the reunion had arrived that spring and sat on the table beside the front door for months, alongside an enormous mound of flyers and unopened junk mail, with stray gloves and ballpoint pens interspersed. Something called the Dunsmuir Alumni Committee had organized these things every few years for the last decade. He and Carol had snorted about them, wondering whose lives were so dull that their high school years seemed like a good thing to dwell upon. Who, that is, had never made it out of Dunsmuir and oh my God, could you imagine that? said the new residents of southern Ontario in their lovely new vinyl-sided signature residence, at the end of an attractive traffic-slowing cul-de-sac.

It seemed incomprehensible to Jim now that he had ever imagined his life to be more interesting than anyone else's. They lived in Etobicoke, just outside of Toronto. Which had many more expensive coffee shops and several imported furniture dealers, it was true, but look at what he had become there—the withdrawn bookkeeper of Robinson's Plumbing Supply. Preoccupied with computer games and Internet sex sites. As pale and soft as Oreo cookie filling. A man sandwiched between two chocolate wafers.

He had thought that he would recognize more people here. But while the place was staggeringly unchanged, he didn't remember a soul. Jim had imagined Margaret Huebsch would be here, in the bar beside Nancy Gustafson and Phillip Campbell, all laughing loudly and confident of the string of victories that lay in their futures and immediate pasts, stretching from hockey rinks to summer cabins, graduate schools or eponymous car dealerships, to security and the admiration of all.

They weren't, of course, nor was anyone else at all that Jim had ever seen before. He remembered whole nights spent at exactly this table in the Wagon Wheel, chipping exactly this paint with his thumbnail. He had thought that coming here would help him get back on track, resume the direction that he ought to have been headed these last half-dozen, dozen, dozen and a half, years. It occurred to him now that perhaps he had never actually ever gotten off track, that he was now where he had been headed, twenty years previously.

Jim missed his wife. He drank his rye slowly. He hadn't been up to that life, with that family, that situation, but he missed Carol. He didn't blame her for taking off. They both had, after all. She had thought Dunsmuir a hilarious town, and would have enjoyed the reunion in an ironic way. He had learned irony from her. She had never lived outside of Toronto, and for her irony was like faith. A whole way of looking at the world. Viewed through that lens, Garth Brooks, for instance, became entertaining rather than inevitable. Seagram's Five Star became something to laugh about. In Dunsmuir, among Dunsmuirites, Five Star was no joking matter. Dunsmuir was generally a no-go zone for irony. Goddammit.

Jim shook his head. He lived in Etobicoke.

Lester walked into the Wagon Wheel and surveyed the thin crowd, recognizing a half-dozen faces he thought he knew for a moment, but did not. Jim saw him walk in and look around expectantly. Jim was sure he would recognize him in a moment but he couldn't quite recall those features buried within that encasement of flesh. Lester approached Jim.

"You must be here for the reunion."

Jim rising, extending his hand. "How could you tell?"

"Body language or something."

"I know what you mean." They exchanged names and thought they remembered one another. Was there a geography class they had both been in? Not sure. Anyway. Seen anyone else you remember? Me neither. Just in tonight.

"In Etobicoke. I work in a plumbing and heating store there. Retail. I, uh, went there to launch my career."

"Huh. I'm up from Rushing River. I've been living there since I finished high school. Work in a bar there. I like it. Nice town."

"Did you know that guy who went over the falls a few years ago and drowned?"

"Vaguely."

"That was crazy."

"Yep."

"Does anyone ever try that anymore?"

"No."

"I guess they were put off by that attempt. I heard he had made quite a barrel for himself. I guess if he didn't make it in that thing, no one could."

"I think that's the general impression."

"Did it break up or flood or what?"

"The barrel?"

"Yeah."

"I'm not sure of the details."

"Interesting."

"Stupid."

"I suppose. Still, you can't help admiring him a little."

"I guess."

"So have you been back here since you left?"

"Not for more than a few hours."

"Why did you decide to come to this?"

"I'm not sure. Curiosity, I suppose."

"About our classmates."

"Yeah, or something. To see how much I've aged, maybe."

"Them, you mean."

"Yeah."

Albert sat at the Riverside Grill eating a grilled cheese sandwich. He recalled the elderly Ukrainian man who had taken his order and prepared his sandwich. He had come here often to eat, especially on his lunch breaks from the Esso station, after the Dairy Queen had become too embarrassing.

He lived now in Toronto and hadn't been back to Dunsmuir in six years. Each Christmas he had dithered over whether or not to come home to his parents, but in the end had never managed to summon up sufficient strength. In Toronto he worked in a publishing house as a copy editor. His company specialized in coffee-table books, and he had flipped through proofs of many aerial studies of the prairies, glowing amber with rising or falling light. How beautiful this part of the world seemed to him then, in his office overlooking that tolerant and anonymous city. His lover, a Portuguese man named João, had not come with him. His observation, about the coffee-table books and nostalgic exercises such as this reunion, was that beauty lives in representations more vibrantly than it does in the actual. Albert thought this an unnecessarily pessimistic idea. In response, João showed him photographs of Portugal and told him stories of his childhood there.

The Ukrainian man's wife arrived and she smiled at Albert, not recognizing him after all, and she and her husband disappeared into the kitchen. Albert was the only other person in the Riverside Grill that afternoon. He wore a camel coat over an expensive black sweater, and his shoes gleamed self-consciously beneath the table.

His brother had not showed up yet, which hadn't surprised him. Albert had checked with his parents and on his voice mail, and there was no word from him. Robert had said he was coming a dozen times over the previous three months, but he had said it in the hurried way that Albert recognized from years of self-absorbed fiascos. His brother was in Montreal, supposedly doing another fellowship. He had constructed his life around grant applications, which, it appeared, he was quite adept at writing. There had been a winter in Paris and a couple more in Toronto and many years of lucrative lounging in Montreal. After many, many attempts to understand, Albert had stopped asking Robert to explain what he was working on, exactly. His brother had not noticed this yet, but would soon, presumably. Albert suspected that his success with grant applications lay in that same doggedness.

Albert's reasons for coming to the reunion were as opaque as he suspected those of the other attendees were; in high school he had had a crush on a boy named James Wilson and in subsequent years had heard from mutual friends—Cora, among others—that James had come out and was living in Vancouver. For many years Albert had wanted to meet this man. They had come from the same place, after all, and each had endured his own circumstances privately, certain that he was unique. Albert thought about the movie scene, the one with the man in the hole, tapping away at the wall with his spoon, happy when he finally heard someone tap back. One of the invitation flyers he had received listed confirmed attendees and Wilson's name had been on it. Albert had decided to go. If Wilson could go, Albert could, he figured. It was like a dare. And anyway, his brother was coming for sure, he had said.

Cora checked into a room above the Wagon Wheel Restaurant, where she had lived during her last year of high school. She left home as a consequence of domestic discord, like industrial solvent in the eyes, and her own strength of will, which had found its full expression early in life. She and Albert had spent many hours up here—she wasn't sure if this was the actual room she had had but it certainly could have been—and the television, carpet, and wall covering (she hestitated to call it wallpaper, it was more like a rind) had remained unaltered from her time here.

She was not unaltered, though; she had not quite appreciated the scope and nature of how she had changed until the drive up here. It was, oddly, the first time she had ever really considered what she was becoming, had become, living there in Pigeon River, working hard and known by everyone. She served the purposes of the town, clearly. She was a part of it, and it was assumed that she would remain there for many years yet. Neither Cora nor anyone else had reason to doubt that. It wasn't so odd. All the women in her extended family had constructed lives around taking care of a group of people—generally a smaller group than a full town, admittedly, but the concept was the same. She had conceived of herself as being fundamentally different from her mother, aunts, and sisters but that, it appeared, was only vanity.

There was meaning and worth to what she did; she had told herself this enough times that she stopped challenging the point. It was only when she stopped viewing herself from afar that the limitations of this life revealed themselves to her.

The first few years, she had driven into the city every couple of months, for the weekend. She went to art films and galleries and hung out at bars. She took people back to her hotel room with her. In the morning she ordered room-service breakfast and exchanged demographic information. There had been a couple of men, and a woman, who had delighted her. The subsequent pattern of petering-out correspondence wore on her a little, and she stopped doing this so much. It seemed slight to dwell upon what she missed: coffee of a certain strength, restaurant meals, bookstores, a sense of urgency, unselfconscious beauty, sex. Sex.

Sex. The television noises coming into her room were unattenuated by their passage through the few millimetres of particleboard and everyone adjoining her was watching something that was shot in poorly lit video, with monotonous musical tracks and sets that might possibly have seemed plausible in Miami in 1987 but not subsequently or elsewhere. That was the loosest approximation of what she longed for, but it was not unrelated. To just know desire again would be almost enough. Uncooked want, either hers or someone else's. She prodded herself. Nothing.

She walked out into the night, locking her door behind her, and wondering for a moment whether there was any point to that. It might reduce the number of drunks who would otherwise pass out on the bed, she concluded, and walked down the stairs into the prairie evening.

This part of the prairies serves as a feedlot and nursery for the cities: its young people leave these places for grey and various regional centres in the east, and within a dozen years of high school, Cora, who had imagined herself the least likely to remain here, was one of only a couple dozen of her graduating class to live here still— Pigeon River being Dunsmuir, in every beer-bottled and self-righteous way she could think of. She disliked the old woman she envisioned Pigeon River as, but she liked tending her.

She walked· past the Riverside Grill and looked inside. At the table nearest the window was Paul Joly, whom she did not recognize, and Daphne Hainscotter, whom she did, barely. She stopped and waved. They could not have been more obviously from the city if they had been wearing tails. There was a child with them. Cora remembered hearing about Daphne's having a baby but had thought the father was uninvolved. They looked up, finally, and stared, smiling hesitantly.

Cora ordered a milkshake. They were nearly finished with their uneaten sandwiches, but the boy, a five-year-old named Richmond, was very pleased with his french fries. It had taken a moment for Daphne to place her. Paul and Daphne had met at a gastroenterology update in Denver, imagine that, and were now living in Montreal.

"Pigeon River is close to where I was posted when I was in the army," Paul said.

"Shilo?"

"Ten of the three longest years of my life."

"When were you there?"

"Right after medical school."

"Wasn't there an accident around then, some artillery misfire or something?"

"Maybe after I left. . . ."

"Could be, was a while ago."

The Meet 'n' Greet was held in the gymnasium. There was a thin crowd of people who mostly kept their distance. Daphne and Cora found one another smiling insincerely and wishing they were elsewhere. The boy was sick, from the french fries perhaps, and he and Paul were back at the hotel room. There was baby-sitting available but Richmond was vomiting a great deal, Daphne explained. Cora nodded.

"Listen," Cora asked, "how was your time in the Arctic? I heard you were up there and tried to call you a few times, to find out what the work situation was like up there, but never got ahold of you. Did you like it?"

"It was amazing work," Daphne said reverentially, trying to gauge whether or not Cora had heard of the trouble she got into up there. "It's tough, though, working without any backup at all. When things get out of hand there's no one you can call." She looked at Cora. "Sometimes they did get out of hand."

"I heard."

"I figured."

"Things work out, though, huh?"

"Yeah."

"I saw you once in that sports bar."

"Yeah."

"Could have been any of us."

"Paul doesn't know much about all that."

"No problem."

After the Meet 'n' Greet there was a meal and dance at the Dunsmuir and District Community Hall. Jim sat between Cora and Lester, each of them there alone and trying to remember one another. Lester recalled Cora through her affiliation with his friend Bob's twin brother, but Cora couldn't place either of them. Jim, it appeared, had walked through high school both invisible and entirely, but unknowingly, blind. He recalled almost no one at all, and the few friends whose names he could remember had not come to the reunion. He wondered why his wife had stayed with him as long as she did.

James Wilson did not appear at the Meet 'n' Greet, had not, actually, shown up or registered, notwithstanding his confirmation of his attendance more than four months ago. Albert left a few minutes after his conversation with the lacquered woman at the information table, the one who asked him where he had bought his coat, and if he went to a tanning salon or was that natural. He returned to his motel room and packed his bag, but he was too tired to leave just then and the hotel room was too oppressive to spend the evening in.

When Albert arrived halfway through the meal, a place was found for him across the hall from Cora. A plate of rewarmed food was set before him and even from her seat Cora could hear the apologies. She grinned as she looked at him, willing him to see her, but he was preoccupied with his tablemates, each of whom had noisily made room for him, standing and shifting their chairs and welcoming him to their table with toothless little smiles.

Jim remembered Albert—at last, somebody to prove he wasn't in the wrong town. He had sat behind Albert in a Social Studies class and spent a year copying down his answers on exam sheets. It was their only interchange; they had never spoken, so far as Jim could recall. The rest of these people were as much strangers to him now as, he supposed, they must have been twenty years previously. How could that be? He tried to remember who he had expected or hoped to see here, why he had wanted to come. He could come up with no names. The only face he knew was Albert's, and he knew the back of his head better yet. He was in trouble even then. A pity, he thought, that his state wasn't more easily recognizable at the outset. Save everyone a lot of grief.

"Hey, isn't that Albert?" he said to Cora, who was looking that way anyway.

"Yeah, I'm pretty sure," she said, and looked down at her plate. Lester lifted his eyes up and off his and, peering, spotted Albert.

"So now it's not just us three, here by ourselves," he said. "That's a relief." Albert looked up and over at the three of them, looking over at him. There was a long puzzled stare, and then a grin broke over his face like a cracked egg. Lester waved demurely. Jim wagged his fingers. Cora just smiled and smiled.

Mitchell Garson was sitting beside his wife at the far end of the hall, and he was discussing the matter of the interprovincial trade barriers with confidence and volume. Beside him were Daphne Hainscotter and Paul Joly.

Garson was dominating the admittedly thin conversation and apparently seemed unaware that he was sitting with physicians. They both pretended to listen and tried to think of a way of relating interprovincial trade barriers to the subject of their professions, but neither of them could come up with anything. Good God, it sounded like the man was thinking of running for parliament.

Garson, always fleshy, was now more so, though not yet so much that he was feeble. He was the sort of man who protests that the height-weight tables just don't apply to him, care to arm wrestle? In another context, his companions would have told him he was destined for a diabetic and dreadful early demise, but they couldn't quite seem to find an opening.

Lester spotted Mitchell Garson first. He had not seen him since his right hand had been broken in four places on Albert's face, ending his major junior hockey prospects. Cora saw him looking and followed his eyes.

There was then a series of speeches and skits that the reunion committee (predictable names and faces, hardly changed in their perky good cheer or their choice of sweaters from two decades ago) had prepared. Fond remembrances of dead teachers and anecdotes of never-before-revealed student council hijinks were shared with all and polite applause rang out. There was a cash bar, and many of the balding and falsely garrulous men ducked and shuffled desperately, cycling between it and their seats. Every time Cora looked over, Albert's companions seemed to be sliding another rye and ginger in a plastic glass to him. Paul Joly was doing the same; he and Mitchell Garson were alternating rounds. It seemed to Paul that he was in the officers' mess in Shilo again, twenty-five and bored to the point of paralysis, vaguely aware of the capacity of stupidity to disseminate itself like a slow virus. Infecting and then inexorably chewing away at people who once showed promise.

Lester and Jim had noticed Cora's preoccupation with Albert and assumed the matter to be as simple as they imagined it. They encouraged her the way they had once encouraged their friends when they were teenagers. Lester and Jim realized that neither had climbed appreciably in social rank since they had last eaten doughy chicken in this room, and, in consequence, they possessed an optimism regarding improbable desires that had never been much tested by experience. Jim found himself wishing he had known Lester before. He thought that they could have been friends.

Lester was just as drunk as Jim and he felt an affection develop within him for Albert, on Cora's behalf, that was almost uncomfortable. Albert was looking at his watch frequently, between slides being shown, of the science fair award winners of 1978. He was up there, beside a model for wood-alcohol distillation, seventeen years old and desperate. Everyone in the room just wanted to stand up, talk to the two or three people that they had things to say to, and get out of there. Science fair photographs.

And when they stopped, the applause quietened in a moment and the room began flinging itself into little condensates around the walls, knots of former friends and wary spouses. The men, in the suddenly sharper light, had deteriorated more precipitously—prairie bellies and sunburned pates stuck out all over the room. Albert was by far the best-looking man there, his clothes not native to this particular fashion habitat. Eyes followed him as he moved through the room, but none more brightly than Cora's. When they embraced she felt heat in her chest rise up in a manner that on any other day she would have likened to gastroesophageal reflux.

Lester and Jim joined them, embracing Albert with all the love lonely pale men could muster. Albert was puzzled by these two, neither of whom he remembered, but his memory was not perfect.

Cora's story came pouring out in a few minutes right there in front of Jim and Lester, about how she had stayed on in Pigeon River and knew every single person in the community, every single one. And how she lived in the old suicide's wooden house and she had tried to keep horses for a while but it was too much work and suddenly, about six weeks ago or so, she had gotten a little old. And how very fine it was to see him again. Yes, she had received a few cards from him in medical school, meant to reply, but hadn't, too busy or something. Sorry. Shaking her head.

Albert looked at her in wonder.

Paul was heading back to the table with another tray of drinks that Daphne had suggested were not entirely necessary when the lights came on. The aisles were suddenly blocked by clots of middle-aged enthusiasms and he found himself shunted over to one wall, peering around for a lead through the pack. He caught sight of Daphne then, listening indulgently to that bore, and for the first time since they had met, he thought he could imagine where she had come from, what she had been through. He imagined her spending years listening patiently to the boy-versions of Mitchell Garson and the girl-versions of his wife, pretending, in that way of hers, that she was elsewhere. He imagined this place in the winter, just as dreadful as Shilo, but with decades to go before she could get out. The smell of Shilo and Sergeant Martin suddenly filling his nose.

Daphne looked frightened sometimes, out of proportion to circumstances and at odds with her usual disposition, and he imagined that he understood a little bit now. He pictured the places she escaped to while living here: the books she had read, the ideas of grace and self-sufficiency that she had cultivated in herself. He thought he grasped her in a way he had never grasped anyone. He was drunk and he knew that. Cora was talking to a man ten years younger than anyone else in the room. She saw him and waved. She looked hammered, herself. A lead opened up through the crowd.

Mitchell Garson, en route to the washroom, came stumbling through the knot of people collected by the doorway. It was crowded and there were pickle-stained paper plates on the floor and it was easy to stumble. When he collided drunkenly with Albert, the jarring knocked both men nearly to their knees. Albert turned around.

"What was that for?" he gasped.

Mitchell Garson said nothing, but only breathed, cattlelike through his broad face, his little pink tongue on his moist lips. Jim and Lester saw this encounter and froze for a moment. Cora blanched like an egg white. Lester took a step forward. Jim advanced as well, lifting his arms above his head. Mitchell Garson turned and stumbled toward the washroom, still breathing heavily. Albert watched him walk away. After twenty feet Mitchell Garson stopped and turned. Both men opened their mouths. "Who is that?" they each asked of the person nearest to them.

# Acknowledgments

Firstly, I thank my editors, Anne Collins at Random House Canada and Nan Talese at Doubleday. They were both implausibly patient with me over this book, and pushed it and me beyond our natural resting points. I could not be more grateful.

The following people have offered their support and friendship in ways that at one point or another made all the difference: Scott Bell, Sheila Thornton, Bruce Martin, Moni Fricke, Bill McCormack, Kevin Zbuk, Sander van Zanten, Mike Kenyon, Tony Turner, Don Hilton, Pam Orr, Ker Wells, Megan Saunders, Ellen Reid, Angela van Amburg, Matthew Welsch, Martinique Stilwell, Steven Beed, Paul Tough, Donna Morrissey, MoJo and the staff at Frog Hollow, Kevin Oneschuk, Meaghan Stothers, Steve Hunt, Brian Daly, John McMillan, Paul Wilson. And thank you, of course, to Molly and Shauna.